Roots & Branches Series

Idylls
of
Complicity

a novel

Carl Watson

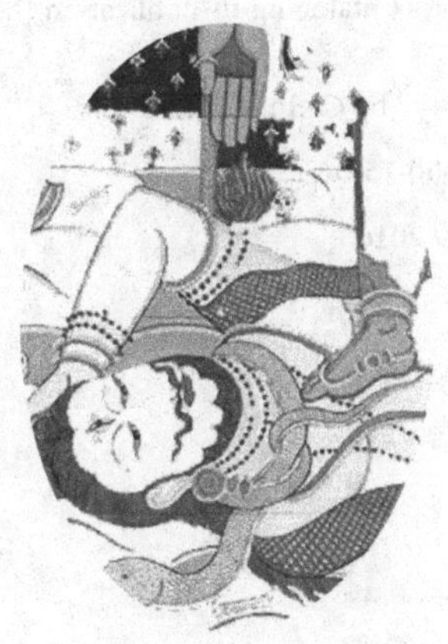

SPUYTEN DUYVIL
New York City

Acknowledgments

A section of Chapter Two of *Idylls of Complicity* was published in Sensitive Skin Magazine. A section of Chapter Ten appeared in *Fortunes du regard*, L'espace Paul Ricard, Paris.

The author wishes to thank the *Maison des Ecrivains et Traducteurs, St. Nazaire, France,* for their generous residency in which much work on this novel was accomplished.

Library of Congress Cataloging-in-Publication Data

Watson, Carl.
Idylls of complicity / by Carl Watson.
pages cm
ISBN 978-1-941550-75-5
I. Title.
PS3573.A8477I49 2016
813'.54--dc23
2015032090

for T. C.

kaler daSa-sahasraaNi
madbhaktaaH saMti bhu-tale
ekavarNaa bhaviSyaMti
madbhakteSu gateSu ca[1]
—the Brahma-vaivarta Purana

ab kaloo aaeiou rae
eik naam bovahu bovahu
an rooth naahee naahee
math bharam bhoolahu bhoolahu[2]
—Guru Granth Sahib Ji, Ang: 1185

---

1 *For 10,000 years of Kali such devotees of Mine will be present on earth. After the departure of My devotees there will be only one varna, Outcaste.*

2 *Now, the Dark Age of Kali Yuga has come./Plant the Naam, the Name of the One Lord./It is not the season to plant other seeds./Do not wander lost in doubt and delusion.*

PROLOGUE

Sophie was into serial killers and true crime. One day I told her I was picked up hitchhiking by John Wayne Gacy on a dark and stormy night down in Bloomington, Indiana, that I jumped out of the car at a stoplight, and that's why I was around to court her today. She jokingly accused me of creating a recovered memory. I said "No, it really happened."

"You wish," she said.

From then on I realized anything I told her would be taken as a metaphor of some repressed desire. It became a private game between us. I once told her how, as kids, we used to vandalize local graveyards—that this was a way of trivializing death. We'd use the skulls in fertility rituals. Teenagers from our town had a reputation—acclimated to the taste of death, we could stomach anything and take pleasure from it.

To me it didn't matter if the stories were true. Under an ochre blanket of sulfured sky, cooled by west winds bearing the stench of slaughtered livestock, surrounded by rivers whose fumes stung our eyes—it was necessary to dream. Beer-bellied bottom-makers dreamed of flipping burgers at backyard barbecues while a candy-colored aviary warbled and the grey Gary trees feigned green. The bottom-makers' daughters dreamed of horses, hot cars, maybe California, while the Calumet River plied its course through the reclaimed swamps.

It was no Danube, no Ganges, no Seine. You couldn't bathe or play the troubadour on its banks, so you told stories to ante up the drama.

A lot of the story I'm about to tell took place in bars—or rather the conversations in them—all connected through wormholes of time and space like umbilical cords between words and events, making random causation seem like narrative fate, which is how I ended up on Falkland Road in Bombay, at a place called the Rava Lounge. The Rava is at the end of the line on Falkland Road. It's not a typical Indian bar—and by that I mean it's not all men. It's frequented by merchants, wayfarers, prostitutes—the spillover from the Olympia Cafe down the street. But the Rava is sparsely populated and far less ornate. It's got the ceiling fans, running water, all those trappings—a cool retreat.

I could describe it as a respite from the howling outside of the fifty-rupee prostitutes in their cages, and the din of the donkey carts, water-bearers and chai-wallahs, but the description would be a cliché. You might even accuse me of copying the cliché from some travel brochure or an adventure novel. But clichés are often true, if unsettling. This is the northside of Bombay after all, not the northside of Paris or even Istanbul. You have to decide what you want: existentialism, cold-war intrigue, or post-colonial alienation in a third-world red-light district.

I was drinking one of those big cold bottles of Lord Ganesha Lager. An elephant head on a man's body, a myth ending as an icon on a beer bottle, and it was making friendly kung-fu signs at me, or semaphores if you will, as if trying to guide my flighty mind like an errant aircraft onto the tarmac of an alcoholic stupor, or at least a bout of self-interrogation. Because, to tell the truth, I didn't know what I was doing back there or even why I thought Sophie would be alive. Sophie Marie. I took a drink and thought her name out loud like a punctuation mark to resolve the rambling thoughts that led up to her. I don't know why; it was a stupid idea. Maybe if I had a photo archive in my head I could compare the memories, put this idea up against that one, rate them for felicity, maybe. But this isn't the "maybe" world anymore. Besides, I don't remember anything that clearly. Maybe it's the parasites infecting my mind.

I'd only been in Bombay a couple days and I already knew something was living inside me. Whether it was self-doubt or a colony of worms, I couldn't be sure. Parasitism can be subtle, grandiose, even elegant. Tapeworms longer than the Sears Tower have been discovered in human intestines. There are miniscule mites living in your eyelids right now. Tiny butterflies are said to move through the vast cavities of our bodies, living off the fat that pads our organs. In fact, what we think is our body is mostly made of other animals. People are walking ecosystems, war zones for collective energies and emotions that have nothing to do with them. Selfish genes and sexual desire are certainly part of it.

I read somewhere, that back in the dim history of dark waters and one-celled organisms, sexuality actually evolved as a strategy for parasite resistance. It's both ironic and odd then, how in this process, sex creates or is related to the metaphor of the human heart, another kind of parasite. I know it's corny, and possibly Freudian, to say so. But if you ask me, this thing, this heart, doesn't even really exist the way we usually refer to it. It's a stand-in for something undefined. Lust translated as love? The demon of self-regard? The fact that it's all abstraction does not stop the hunger. We have to die of something. Lots of animals form intense relationships with the thing that will kill them. Such fatalism is my forte. But not mine alone.

Back at the Rava Lounge, I contemplate the scorpion fight I watched earlier, on a nearby street corner. Sometimes in the heat of fighting the scorpion stings itself. It's funny how I often think of Sophie when I witness such war-like spectacles: a man and a woman punching each other in the street, an argument in a distant window. I've seen cockfights and fistfights. Drunks throwing air punches in Madison Street dives. In an Uptown alley once I saw two hillbilly women going after each other with broken bottles. In every case, I think how close I came to that fire, and how I failed.

Sophie and I did fight, but be it for a prize or for mere survival, who could tell. The shrink said "*folie a deux.*" The cop called it codependency when the neighbors finally reported us. Sophie said it was just my lack of respect for her mercurial charms. Funny how you can spend years with a woman thinking you're getting somewhere. A big part of you disappears in the process.

When you finally do walk away you feel depleted but free, so you keep walking.

See, I'm rambling again. I guess it's the music, the Indian music, the strange tonic scales and rhythms. I'm not used to it and it throws me off, puts my thinking on an odd track. I recall suspicious memories. Music is this powerful. But, in truth, smell is the most primal, catalyst of our past. And here in this bar on Falkland Road, I'm assaulted by a parade of stenches and sweet scents: black pepper, cumin, curry, raw sugar, something septic, and something else slightly sweet and deep that brings to mind Sophie's perfume.

Hindus believe that we are presently living in the fourth stage of the universe, known as the Kali Yuga, with virtue at its lowest ebb and the human lifespan at its shortest. (This is not Kali Ma but the demon Kali of the Kalki Purana and the Mahabarata) The Kali Yuga is an evil time and it's meant to be—they call it "the last roll of the dice. They say, at the end of the Kali age, doomsday will arrive in the form of a mare at the bottom of the ocean. Inextinguishable flames will issue from her mouth. It's a great picture, a catastrophic vision. And Sophie always did believe in some kind of cataclysm of the metaphysical sort as a deserved human come-uppance. It was behind her every extravagant gesture, like the sorrow that hides behind laughter. Or maybe it was just an act, a pose to hook a pessimistic man. Well, if it was, it worked. Indeed, my road to Sophie and beyond was paved with characters that would have loved to warn me off it. Kathe and Bernadette,

Rajinder and Boggs and Arnaud. And Sonny—Sonny Valentine, a name that sounds like a bad joke when you first hear it.

The men seem just devices now. As to the women, I can still hear each one. I can see their petticoats flouncing in a vision, as their legs kick high in a can-can dance staged as if in the muzzle of a gun. Sophie was gone now. My business was to make sense of her disappearance—figure how and why it happened. I was never very good at that. I *was* good at pointing out other people's faults, though. And that's not something that makes you popular. Which is part of the reason I was in Bombay, at the Rava Lounge, and not at Studio 54. I was drinking a cold Lord Ganesha Lager. You can't get it anywhere else. The Lager of the God of Good Fortune. I was gonna need some of that.

Part One

The messengers said to the students,
"Let our offering all be for obtaining salt"
Salt is what they called Sophia.
Without salt no offering is acceptable.
But Sophia is barren. She has no child,
And so she is called a trace of salt.
Yet wherever others are will be the holy spirit.
Her children are many.
                    —The Gospel of Philip

When Sophia saw what her desire had wrought,
    it changed into the figure of a snake with the face of a lion.
Its eyes were like flashing bolts of lightning.
She cast it to a distance and surrounded it with a bright
    cloud and put a throne in the middle of the cloud so that
    no one would see it except the holy spirit, who is called the
    mother of the living.
She named her offspring Yaldabaoth and it was to make
    fools of men.
              —The Fall of Sophia, The Secret Book of John

(one)

It's not always easy to figure out where it begins, or even *if* it does. You have to finally pick a spot and say "go." I pick Bernadette just because it's convenient. Truth be told, it all boils down to a large measure of accident and a minimum of intention. You go to a show, a bar, a "soiree" at some poseur's apartment, you get invited to a poet's loft party; before you know it you're running with a hi-tone crowd. Bernadette seemed out of my league at first. But that only made it normal.

Actually, the Bernadette affair started as an unrequited crush on another woman. Her name was Annie Valdez. I saw her unattended at a party, across the room. I started to walk over. Maybe that shocked her. Maybe she was drunk. But subtly, if unconsciously backing away from my lurid approach, she stumbled and fell into a black glass coffee table. The glass broke and cut her face. It was a mess, not to mention embarrassing for everyone. I picked a couple glass chips like watermelon seeds out of her red cheek. Another friend would drive her to the hospital.

Before she left, Annie said she hoped we could meet again under different circumstances. I agreed, as I led her to the stairs. Maybe we could have had something. The incident didn't stop the party at all. People were soon dancing. The Pretenders, I think, were on the turntable. The woman whose party it was, the hostess, Kathe, thanked me. Apparently she thought I had some kind of concern for people and that was a good thing—there were so few concerned people around. This misconception got me invited to another party, the next weekend, with Kathe as a sort of unofficial consort.

It was one of those Wicker Park loft affairs: large and somewhat anonymous. It gave us room to get to know each other, sitting in an out-of-the-way corner in relation to the general festivities. Kathe was a neo-Marxist working in advertising—direct mail actually, but she pretended it was mid-level retail and that it was a "creative" position. She understood the hard- and soft-sell concepts of life and the importance of flattering the buyer's ego. I thought I had met someone like her before, but it turns out it actually *was* her, just an earlier version. It was Sarah's ex-boyfriend's ex-girlfriend who knew this guy who was going out with Kathe and who used to tell stories about how ambitious she was and the conflict between her much touted feminist independence and her obsessive desire to trap a husband. So we had mutual friends. She had even been to my place once, hanging on the arm of some low-level photographer for a liberal weekly. The photographer was delivering a used air-conditioner to me that someone else didn't want. Kathe was riding along. She looked different back then.

Considering the circumstances of our knowing each other, it seemed natural to transfer my original Annie-affections to Kathe. It might sound defensive, but it was more than solvency and upward social mobility that attracted me, although I'd have trouble putting my finger on it. One night we were dining at a candlelight restaurant when it struck me that I was sexually drawn to her as well, something I hadn't actually noticed before. I don't tend to trust sexual attraction because it's the kind of motive you can fool yourself into when you really have something financial on your mind. But even if the sexuality starts as a side effect, it can eventually usurp the original agenda. Certain parts of the brain go numb. Ambition, judgment—all fall by the wayside. Sadly, eventually, so does the sex. The fallout can last for years. One day you wake and wonder why the hell you ever thought this person was a good idea. Needless to say, we started keeping company.

Kathe and her friends did things like go to art galleries, and talk about super-realism, neo-expressionism, post-hedonism (everything was hyphenated in those days). They were mostly Ph.D. candidates who dabbled in the crrent popular culture. They used words like "problematic" and "paradigmatic" and "semiotic" and "Derridean." It was a highly social circle and the number of people you knew was a sign of your potency within it. But there was danger as well. You could get confused, forget whose friend was whose and/or whether you were supposed to like so-and-so or not. Your allegiances could, and often needed to, shift in regard to your surroundings, like a servile puppet manipulated by lines of subtle obligations you were not immediately aware of.

To protect herself, Kathe obsessively categorized her personal life. Everything and everyone had a place and time; think of tools hanging neatly on hooks in a pegboard in some anal-retentive's garage, or different sizes and colors of buttons in the little plastic drawers of a speed-freak seamstress. She was afraid if she mixed friends incongruously they would fight. In those days everyone's personality was threatened and delicate, and fighting was one way to advertise that fact while, at the same time, seeming to deny it. It may have been cool to have anxieties, but I think Kathe's anxieties were based more on what such a fight would reveal about her—how she would react, and who she would defend if forced to take sides. She told me she had a completely different personality with different people and didn't want to get caught in any conflict of selves because she was "probably" schizophrenic. I said parties were "probably" a bad idea then. Not really, she said, because she was a masochist, too. The comment was supposed to be funny, but humor was an odd fit on her.

Kathe did have an odd mix of friends. She had her low-rent friends to whom she played the role of nutty yuppie. She had her advertising and catalogue-writing friends to whom she was the token "freak" in the copy department. She had her jazz friends and her folk friends, and her post-modern deconstruction literati friends. Somehow she did manage to keep them in their respective compartments. And then there were strays, people who drifted in and out of certain scenes, but were never really part of anything. I was one of those strays and so was Bernadette. Bernadette was a name I'd heard in conversation, but to whom I'd never been able to attach a face.

Not everybody got to meet Bernadette. Kathe kept her in a social drawer so to speak. I remember the first time I saw her. A month or so had gone by and Kathe was having a party. I arrived late. Kathe was waving her arms around in an argument about whether capitalism, birth control or the atom bomb had the greatest effect on modern romance. "Love under capitalism is nothing but exchange value," she said. "Dating is shopping." Somebody nodded in agreement. Kathe went on, "A boyfriend is really, you know, like an expensive dog or a tailored suit—you wear what makes you look good." She was on a roll. I was across the room, but I could hear her, which seemed odd. But what was odder was the visual impression that accompanied the conversation. It was as if Kathe, as she spoke, had four arms instead of two. She was facing my direction speaking to some guy in a sweater. "The threat of mass destruction changed everything," she was saying. Then Bernadette stepped out from behind her, and I realized there were two people, as if one had been born from the other's backside. It was a trick of the angle and I was pretty sure I was the only one who saw it.

Bernadette seemed like someone worth knowing, even at that distance, and we shared a half-avoided but curious glance. To her credit, Kathe tried to derail our possible future friendship by routing Berny to a far corner of the room. I found her anyway, at least long enough to introduce myself and hear her laugh. It was a good laugh—solid and sardonic, but not lacking sympathy. But then she had to leave suddenly and our meeting was cut short.

For the next month or so Bernadette would appear and disappear. I'd see her at Amvets, or at a bookstore. I never got a good fix on her, however. But I was usually with Kathe on these occasions, which I'm sure had something to do with it. And then there were Kathe's oft-dropped hints about their near-lesbian familiarity, and the less than subtle mentions of Bernadette's track record of crushing men for laughs. There was something about drugs and mental instability and time spent in institutions. At some point I had to question Kathe's game. Working in the world of consumer manipulation, she should certainly have known that Bernadette would become the forbidden door I longed to open.

One thing was true—there was a bond between the two. If opposites attract, maybe that was part of it. While Kathe was dishwater blonde with brown eyes, Bernadette was brunette verging on auburn with muddy green eyes like dirty moss. Sometimes Kathe said Berny was her evil twin. Maybe Kathe was jealous, or maybe she was afraid of the fact I might like the bad side of her better.

This hide and seek went on until the day of the funeral. A poet friend of theirs had died from "complications." After the service, we all went over to the Club Lucky dining room to drink and read the dead poet's poems. It was a sort of memorial, the intention being to pretend we cared a lot about the dead guy while laying into the free buffet. Apparently some people did care. In fact, a subtle "caring competition" seemed to be going on in which the participants spoke in faltering voices, feigned emotional distraction, and pinched long-dormant nerves in order to produce appropriate facial expressions, and, in some cases, actual tears. The prize was being able to feel like you were a good person after all and not just another dilettante bolstering your ego or your social status. I dropped out early. I didn't really know the guy anyway. Besides, I always have trouble at funerals, something akin to inappropriate laughter.

Bernadette apparently had a similar problem. She was breaking the ice among the direct-mail crowd by telling dead-poet drinking stories. She had a right after all—she actually liked the guy and understood him and saw him as more than a social token. Still, people shook their heads in disgust—exactly the response Berny wanted. I caught her eye. She smiled. That was my signal. I looked around. Kathe was busy juggling personalities in front of a rapt audience—this was an event she had no control over and she had some explaining to do. Berny and I stole away to the cold-cut table for sandwiches and developed a rapport based on our mutual appreciation of Kathe's duplicity, as well as the shallow waters we seemed to be drowning in. From then on we were pretty good friends.

Now, just to make the world a little smaller, it turned out there was another connection. Bernadette was originally a friend with my old pal, James D. They'd met professionally years before I knew either one of them. Bernadette had a job at the local Humane Society. Part of her duties included putting down the feral dogs caught prowling the vacant lots and alleys of Humbolt Park and West Town. James worked for some private public health agency. His job was killing pigeons to keep them from fouling fancy office facades. James used the term "public nuisance." He had a business card—Jameson D. Powers, Urban Ornithologist. It was funny because it was supposed to be.

He and Bernadette met at a convention for people who killed unwanted animals. Apparently they weren't so comfortable with their professions and eventually ended up in the same rehab program. That was the beginning of their falling out: the in-house encounter group sessions; the out-of-house moral quibbling, the constant baiting to pick up. Anyway, I met James D. some time later. I didn't know they had ever even known each other, but talking to Berny it was suddenly obvious. They were both addicts once. They were both nuisances. And they were both nuisance-killers. Indeed, they were once friends. Now they wouldn't talk to each other. I, however, talked to both of them. And when I did, they always asked about each other.

Berny went back to her old job. James went into house painting. I sometimes worked with him. We'd talk about Tennessee Williams and Genet, his favorite writers. Once, we went to a bar after work, just off North Ave. on a gentrifying block. We ran out of cash. James stepped out of the bar and robbed the first white guy he saw. It was posed as a joke, but it worked. We were both covered with white and brick-red paint. And there was James D. in the shadow of the high rises of Cabrini Green, threatening some lost office worker with a hammer. "Buy this hammer or die," he said. He only wanted ten bucks and the guy gave it to him. James said thanks, gave the guy the hammer and asked him to join us. The guy just stood there confused. I didn't go drinking with James anymore after that. I did go to Bernadette's house sometimes to share a bottle on a long afternoon. It was all very civilized. We would listen to opera and sip some untried bourbon from Zimmerman's premium shelf. We alternated on who brought the bottle.

Bernadette had a lot of books, which I liked—the three copies of the PDR were most notable, along with other medical and psychological classics like *Psychopathia Sexualis* and Cesare's *L'uomo delinquente*. There were some novels—*Melmoth the Wanderer*, *The Mysteries of Udolpho*. There were biographies of opera singers and the de rigeur trendy philosophy—Foucault, Longinus, Kant, Burke. Maybe she *was* smart. However, I don't trust bookshelves; they're too easy to fake.

I do trust video collections. Her video shelf, though small, was large for the time—gore, horror, slasher, splatter. Some noir. Mostly bootlegs. She had medical documentaries on various mutations and syndromes. She even had a personal copy of *Signal 30*. I don't know where she got that. She liked the blue and bleeding bodies of the teenage car-crash victims—but with the soundtrack off, listening to opera instead. She believed that slasher and gore films like this were the modern-day secular equivalent to the medieval saint's lives in which various devout Christians were maimed, tortured, and torn apart only to achieve redemption and eternal bliss. In this modern version though, bliss was evasive.

Apparently, next to carnage and gothic literature, Berny loved opera. She talked about irony and sarcasm in Mozart and leitmotifs in Debussy. One of her heroes was Richard Wagner. Another was Maria Callas, an example, she said, of pure will sabotaged by romantic plurality, a protean shape-shifter from another planet who went about reviving the dead bel canto repertoire so she could spend her career playing mad women. Berny's monologues were over my head, but the music I could understand, or pretend to. In response to some Callas arias she once played, I said the voice had a galvanized steel shrill quality, like a cat scratching on a metal plate in the back of my neck. It made the hair in my ears quiver, and I wasn't sure I enjoyed it. Berny agreed, but said it wasn't the singing so much as the drama that mattered, and that it was through these canned histrionics, this codified acting out, that we could escape the terror of freedom. I just nodded.

Indeed, Bernadette was something of a drama queen herself. Her life, as she told it, was a mess looking for a plot. She was really from somewhere else, but she couldn't go back there, so she was in Chicago, but she wouldn't say if it was permanent. She could always seem one way when she was really another. Like doors in a giant endless house, you kept opening new ones, finding out one more bizarre or difficult fact about her life, and it was almost always something you didn't want to know. But as much as you did know, it never seemed like you knew anything. For whether on purpose or not, she was vague about much of it: the childhood mental problems, the stepfather, the years in Texas, those hints about a brother-in-law in the pen, the sort-of sometime-boyfriend who kept showing up in town. It just went on and on.

Sometimes these stories would partially surface from the mixmaster of her monologues on this or that aspect of culture, history and capitalism. That is to say, she'd be going on some political diatribe, and then maybe a word would trigger a supposedly related story. Or the story might float up, just like that, unexpectedly but not unnaturally, like a chattering skeleton strapped to an easy chair rising up in a bubbling whirlpool of psychological swill. Times like that you might even think you had a clue as to who she was—there was something you could actually see—but then that easy chair and that skeleton would disappear again just as quickly, and you'd be lost, sitting across the table from a very strange woman with opaque eyes. I'd like to say those eyes were bizarre or exotic, but they weren't. Long ago she must have glassed them over on purpose so as not to let anyone see inside. The blinds were drawn—no one home. But when she wanted to, she could focus on a speck of dust, the tiniest doubt or indecision in your soul, and with a single look she could nail you and make you feel like you didn't know one goddamn thing at all about this world so you better not talk like you did.

Bernadette, however, was perfectly free to talk about

whatever she wanted. And, for a woman who hated clichés she certainly depended on them. She was anti-this and anti-that, anti-everything. She was also a woman who loved fools. She had one boyfriend who could only get off if she was tied up. They stayed together for about a year. She had another boyfriend who filmed himself cutting the word RAGE into his arm with a razor. It was supposed to be performance art, but Berny said the guy was pretty much of an asshole. In fact, she freely admitted that most of her friends were assholes and that it was her special talent, having friends she didn't really like—it took some of the pressure off. She'd given up on Americans, and only dated Europeans. You couldn't read them so easily and being a jerk and being sophisticated were pretty much the same thing with them. Still, it was all flirtation with clichés. Italians were oversexed. Germans were overwrought. The English were just weird.

Amongst her constantly shifting interests were eugenics, cabalism, and Wagnerian sexual fantasy. The great thing about our relationship was that there was never any question of sex. On more than one occasion we got close, but pulled away at the last second, knowing it was a bad road to travel. This repressed carnality allowed us to be more intimate, more comfortable with each other. Sometimes I would walk in on her conducting an air orchestra in her underwear. She didn't care. Other times she would be parading around with a hiball glass in one hand and a riding crop in the other talking about how she was gonna kick some ass in the poetry world if she ever got published. I never understood her poetry at all, or her catatonic rock songs. She claimed it was all modeled on the troubadour school of courtly love, in turn modeled on the Mariology of one St. Bernard, to whom she paid homage by taking the *nom de plume* of Bernadette Clairvaux. I didn't ask for an explanation. I never asked her about the scar either.

I was still seeing Kathe, however, and the closer I got to Bernadette the more Kathe began to hate her. And Bernadette began to hate Kathe in kind. Their unholy sisterhood was becoming unlovely. One thought the other was a drunk. The drunk thought the other was a phony. Somehow I brought out the worst in both of them and that gave me a little thrill. Bernadette always wondered what it was I saw in Kathe and I couldn't tell her. Maybe I was embarrassed to say. Kathe and I were hardly compatible, but I was tired of the kind of work I had been doing—menial jobs, messengers, machine shops, restaurants, etc. Kathe had some kind of small business going and she could give me work in direct mail. It was pretty small on my part, but it was getting more and more alright to be small in this world. People barely judged you anymore *except* by what you could do for them.

Then it all went haywire. I remember the night—an opening down at Randolph Street. A bunch of us were standing outside drinking gin and tonics from plastic cups, expressing our general disregard for commercialism. Bernadette showed up with her newest discovery—a genuine tight-wrapped blonde mill-foreman's daughter from the vast and mysterious Southside. Down there she had been just another isolated white girl, but uptown she was Sophie, actually Sophia Marie Wagner. She even claimed the composer as a distant relative. I'm sure that was part of Berny's attraction. Myself, I thought it unlikely. I knew a lot of Wagners over the years and most of them were hillbillies. But then it turned out her name wasn't really Wagner; it was Walker. Sophie Walker from Canaryville. Part Scottish, part French, part Polish, part Ukrainian, she even claimed a great grandmother named Sophie Beausoleil. All in all, this evolving tissue of indeterminate ancestry made Berny like her even more.

I remember the way Sophie first appeared to me. I'd gone inside for a refill. Berny was standing at the plywood bar in the back room of the gallery. A halo of yellow hair seemed to hover around her head. I thought maybe she had attained some state of grace through the accumulating cocktails. Then, Sophie stepped out from behind her. They were in a heated discussion, and the blonde was pulling away to make her point through vigorous gestures. Then she stopped, dropped one hand and posed. She wore a red dress with weird shoulder pads and silvery blue nylons. She was holding a gold plastic cup of alcohol, and a painting of an angel behind her bestowed a set of temporary wings.

I approached with trepidation. The woman had an ego that hunted like a tentacle. She also had a snake for a tongue and a Southside accent that could melt asphalt. She had delicious plum-colored lips and wore her hair in a bob over small black almond-shaped glasses that suited her oval face. She was in some sense so unfashionable that she was hi-fashion and when she walked she had that high-hipped coltish way of carrying herself, a haughty stance that came off as a dare. Berny made the introduction. Sophie was her new toy, her protege in romantic fatalism. Bernadette collected exotic friends: "here's my friend from Blue Island, here's my friend from the Junaway Jungle," she would say. Indeed, Canaryville might as well have been Eastern Europe or deepest Mexico or some other difficult, obscure place, and I could see this Sophie Walker/ Wagner woman dreaming in the midst of it, a pale lost thing wandering the wide world, a victim of Rimbaud, Baudelaire and Patti Smith. I reached out to shake her hand and Kathe was behind me in a flash. This was exactly what Berny relished—put the two blondes together and see if they would draw blood.

I wanted to watch too, but Bernadette dragged me away. Berny had custody of Tommy Campbell's Honda 350 Scrambler for a week. She handed me a helmet without saying anything and we went for a ride. She was sober even if I was tipsy. We got on the Ryan at Ohio, crossed over at Congress, and came back up Michigan. We were gone all of forty minutes, less than an hour, no time at all in party time. But when we got back, Sophie was dancing in the gallery and Kathe had gone home to trash her own apartment. This was a major turning point. I don't know if she was mad at me, or mad at Berny. I don't guess it mattered much.

(two)

The philosophers of the old romances say, and many specialists today concur, that desire is nothing more than the result of a necessary and continuous projection of the self into others; an unattainable wholeness is represented in an outside object, a body, or a soul. That it must be unreachable is both integral to the relationship and maddening. Some renounce the quest altogether and go shopping. Others retreat into darkness.

Those who monitor behavior in the mental hospitals of Uptown describe a phenomenon in which patients scratch words on their skin with their fingernails or sharp instruments. Some can even make brief defining messages or images appear via the power of the diseased mind alone. Locked away in their heads, relishing their solitude, they seek contact with the outside world, yet they touch no one.

A more social, if trendy, alternative exists in the ancient tribal rite of tattooing. The very longevity of the tattooed image or mark, at first a choice, can, over time begin to seem as if it were prescribed, imposed, imprinted by outside forces. This may, of course, merely be buyer's regret manifesting as identity.

Bernadette had a friend who did tattoos at a place called Kaligraphy Studios on Broadway and Montrose. This friend, Marcus Boggs claimed to be related to the banjo player Dock, although, unlike Dock, he had a strong mystical bent. He believed that the black tattoo ink was the symbolic blood of the Black Goddess Kali, and therefore his art was sacred because it mingled the blood of humans and gods. This idea was the origin of the studio name.

Boggs was in his twenties but looked older, due to his long black beard and his signature style of dress, which was part low-rent rabbi, part 19th century snake-oil salesman. His favorite book was *The Illustrated Man* by Bradbury. He'd loaned it to Berny and one night he came to get it back. Thus started a bullshit session with peculiar consequences.

Sophie was there and steered the conversation toward her interests—serial killers with romantic names: The Green River Strangler, The Mississippi Muskrat, The Sunnyside Slasher. She had just read a criminal case study about a guy from Texas, known as The Red Spider. When they caught him, he claimed his homicidal anxiety was caused by the little red spiders tattooed all over his hands and arms—a kind of post-coital arachnophobia. In any case, he eventually felt he was being attacked by his own skin.

There were lots of examples if you looked for them, Sophie said, of people getting trapped in a metaphor of their own design—bad poets, false gurus, bad lovers, megalomaniacal despots, etc.

Bernadette knew a story about a guy in West Virginia: a man who had thirty-seven butterflies tattooed on his body. He was called Butterfly Bob by the locals. He was also an artist and drove around in an old Ford pick-up truck painted with Victorian fairies. Bob had a collection of small animals preserved in jars. He thought of them as babe magnets. And he was kind of handsome in a West Virginia way. In fact, he managed to pick up women at the local bar. The women were scared, of course, but they were also game. For a while they had the thrill of not knowing whether they'd be dead or alive when the night was over.

One day a gunshot wound from a jealous husband inspired a religious conversion and Bob began to court, and eventually marry, the aging Mexican caretaker of a motel outside Madison. He met her in church and she gave him purpose. It turns out her family was from a small village in Michoacan, the central Mexican state where the Monarchs winter.

"See," Sophie said.

"See what?" I asked.

"See, we all end up victims in the end."

"Victims of what?"

"Of the little things—dreams, obsessions."

Boggs had a theory: tattoos were a lot like paranoia, he said—they begin as fantasies and end as fate. Simply having the words "Born to Raise Hell" on your arm can change your life—you end up killing a bunch of nurses or stabbing your best friend in a card game because you somehow had a picture of yourself doing it. The image becomes a dare forcing a bifurcation in your personal timeline. You might also look back and say it wasn't your fault: "the image made me do it."

People will never stop baiting themselves forward through life with such ideas. "Eventually" in cosmic time becomes "inevitably." But the opposite is also true—events that actually should be expected, end up being a surprise. You just don't know where you're at in the probability continuum.

Which brings me to the story of Robert Arnaud, which was a surprise because it turned out Boggs and I both knew the guy. The summer after high school, me and Arnaud were both flipping burgers at Johnson's Grill on Highway 41. Arnaud was just old enough to drink back then. He quit in the middle of his shift one night and got drunk with this guy Tim "Buck" Cater-toe, or Timbucktoo as we called him. They often went to this motel bar across the road on their break. They met women there and sometimes didn't come back to work.

Timbucktoo eventually got fired. So did Ron Ugly. Ron was the guy who put the butcher knife through the kitchen side door for fun. There was a spate of firings that season. Spinner got fired, and Johnny Flange, two weeks earlier. I got fired myself. But this was all years ago. Then, in the early 80s, Arnaud turned up in the Lakeview neighborhood of Chicago. He and his mother had moved to Albany Park to be near their cousins after his dad died. But Arnaud quickly drifted east, drawn by what he perceived as bohemian freedom. He was the boyfriend of one of Berny's girlfriends so he was sometimes at her place for parties.

Turns out Arnaud knew Boggs via Baltimore back in the day. And lately he'd been going by Kaligraphy to get some work done. It was a big job, full chest—some violent Hindu demon perched on a volcano with fire and fish spewing out of it. The volcano was circled at the base by skulls with worms winding through their eye-sockets.

Arnaud also had, covering each shoulder, these sinister looking swans whose wings seemed to form epaulets. Their elongated necks reached down the biceps, circling around and ending in a toothy beak a few inches past the inside elbow. Then on the inside of each wrist was the small black Q of a curled serpent. Arnaud called them the Nagas of Vedic mythology. The whole tableau had a sort of comic-book quality to it.

I only know all this because one night at Berny's the tattooed people got drunk and started taking off their shirts. After he left, I wondered out loud if Arnaud's torso of violent cataclysm coupled with the Eastern mysticism symbolized a confluence by which he might eventually break on through to another side—a new and better man.

Shortly after that, Bernadette threw me out. She had to work the next day.

But it wasn't even a month later that she called: "You gotta come over, man."

"What?"

"Just come over."

When I got to her place, a few people were there. Boggs told his story. Apparently, a few days earlier, Arnaud came to his shop, acting even weirder than usual—kind of irritable, distracted, and there was a noticeable tremor in his voice. Boggs didn't think much of it because Arnaud was so full of shit anyway and he was always over-dramatizing his emotions.

"So how's Stacey?" Boggs had asked.

"Gettin' on my nerves, as usual," Arnaud replied, pacing around.

"I know what you mean, man."

"No, really, I wanted to fuckin' strangle her this morning. I mean I just could *not* listen to her anymore." He said the word *not* with a certain finality. "I mean I love her but . . . but you know, I have a few drinks or something, I go hang out. So fuckin' what? She's always gotta be on my back."

Boggs tried to placate him. "Yeah, I know. I feel like killing Margaret almost every week. Funny thing is—she's still around. It's our fate man. You know the cliché. Can't live with 'em ...."

"Ain't no good dead either, I guess," Arnaud said, looking at the floor.

Then they had some beers and watched part of the Cub's game. That was a few days ago.

But here's the thing—just that morning, a friend found Stacey in her apartment on West Cuyler. She was naked on the floor, cold and blue with her tongue hanging out, looking very much broken and raped. Cops were asking questions. Arnaud was in the wind. Then Boggs remembered that tremor in Arnaud's voice, the emphatic "*not,*" and said it should have been a clue.

Sophie got riled and blamed Boggs. She said maybe Stacey would still be alive if Boggs hadn't put all that ink on him, turned him into a freak. "Think about it," she said. Sophie was always a little hostile toward Boggs anyway. She thought he was pretentious.

Bernadette came to his defense. She said, "If you're going to think that way, you might as well not speak either. For that matter, better not even get out of bed. There's no telling what sinister chain of events you will start just by your presence in the world. It's the anxiety of influence; it'll freeze you in your tracks."

Boggs just sat there looking worried.

Then one night about a week later I got one of those "two am phone calls" that you know is bad news before you even answer. The phone seems to glow and your hand trembles above the receiver and you feel like you've entered a Hitchcock movie or something. I picked it up anyway, half asleep. It was Boggs, calling from his mother's house in Baltimore.

"What the fuck?" I said, a little irritated.

"I don't know man, I been thinking about this whole thing." He was talking sort of crazily but slow and deliberate.

"Well don't," I said. "Think about *me*, sleeping. I was sleeping, you know."

Boggs ignored me and went on. "I've become like a cameraman of my own future life, which plays out before me like some kind of strange experiment. What I mean is—there is no actual morality, there is only data that we receive, read, and act on. The mind computes, we make the story out of it later."

"Uh huh," I said, not sure what he was getting at.

"I'm telling you, I'm not in it," he said, "I'm always

a couple of steps behind. There's like this slight delay and it's been getting longer recently. If I keep going like this I'll be able to witness my own death and there will still be enough time left for me to …." He didn't finish the sentence.

"I feel that way myself most days," I said. I was being dismissive. "I think you better come back, man. It's not always good to be alone."

He only got more adamant, "No, see. See that's the last sadness: You realize—that if you had known all the time you could have changed things."

"Look, I don't know what you mean, but . . ."

He interrupted me again "You know, I can kind of understand where Arnaud was coming from. God is happy despite the subtle crimes. The universe computes. Everything is on track."

As he spoke, I realized Boggs had an odd tremor to his voice too, probably just exactly like Arnaud had a few weeks earlier. I started to imagine *his* wife's body on the floor, as if the murder scene was being replicated, splitting and growing like a cancer cell in the social imagination.

I asked about his wife. "How's Margaret? She alright?"

He didn't answer. Then I wondered why Boggs was calling me anyway. He was better friends with Berny.

"What's going on, man? You talk to Berny?"

"Yeah. Yeah. No, her phone was out. I'm fine. But listen, if you talk to her, tell Berny I'm okay. I'm not coming back though, not for awhile." There was a voice in the background, a man's voice, a whining voice. It sounded familiar.

"Who's that?" I asked.

"I gotta go," he said.

"Yeah, alright. Sure." Silence.

I phoned Bernadette immediately. Contrary to Boggs's claim, her phone was working. I said I thought Boggs had gone off, and that maybe he even knew where Arnaud was, that he might be in communication with him. I didn't know for sure, but I had this feeling.

"He doesn't know." Her voice was anxious but quiet.

"What do you mean?"

"Because he's here," she whispered.

"What? Where?"

"He's on the couch, in the other room." She hung up.

The rest of the night passed in a blur of sirens and flashing lights, unwanted phone calls and anxious glances. Berny had told the cops, probably because she was afraid. Arnaud slept in holding that night. The rest of us drank but only got morbid. I ended up walking Sophie back to her apartment at about four in the morning. It was raining a little when we reached her building. In the streetlight her skin glowed white and wet, like apple meat contrasting with the red skin of her lips. Her hair lay flat against her head. It gave her that seductive, waifish look which, for some reason, always triggered my savior complex. We were exhausted, depressed, stunned into submissiveness. She thought we should do something about the situation. I wanted to believe we could.

"So what's up with you and Berny?" she asked.

"We're friends. Why?"

"Nothing." She brushed my cheek with those long fingers. "See ya, okay." And that was how it started for us.

I read somewhere that the word Sophia means divine wisdom, that eternal female wisdom which the soul has lost. Bernadette believed that people live up to their names. She had a list to prove this was true. Beths are prudes. Bruces are gay. Bobs are regular guys. Marys are pious, and Marias are always guilty. I don't know about that. I don't know if Sophia was a celestial spouse for anyone, or if she was even wise.

*

I do know that night I had the first of a series of dreams. I was on the road; it was a mountain road, I think, spectacular and misty. There was a feeling of something ominous in the mountain air. Then a low cloud came around the bend in the road ahead—a squat, sweating cloud, a little bigger than a man. It drifted quickly up to me as if with a purpose, like an overcoat or some other piece of clothing that wanted me to wear it. A woman's multiple arms emerged from this cloud. Her hands were holding several implements: an orange, a switchblade, a mirror, a book, a candle, some other stuff. The closer I looked, I could see this cloud was actually a kind of crackling electric mist. Sparking trails of energy were constantly moving across its outer surface, like the distortion on a TV screen when the image is struggling—a face, a torso, a message—something was trying to resolve itself. This resolution did not happen. But there was a soundtrack to the dream. Actually, it was not part of the dream, it came from outside. A high, grating, galvanized voice was singing *"Si, fa core e abbaciciami. Io tutta l'onta mia ti rivelo,"* which translated roughly into, "Watch your back, Frank Payne. The train has left the station."

(three)

I should have known the direction this relationship would take when our first date ended up being a visit to St. John of God's Church on 52nd and Throop in a slightly acid rain. The rendezvous began at the Cermak platform, then moved to the Hung Far Low coffee shop for a late breakfast of boiled black bean buns and Oolong tea. The idea was that no one would see us in such an obscure neighborhood.

It was here Sophie told me about her long-time interest in Virgin Mary sightings. She admitted to being gullible but saw it as a virtue. I said the Virgin was probably a bad role model, especially for teenagers—too obedient, too repressed. Sophie said there could be no philosophy without repression, just as there was no true love that was free of anxiety. I shot back that Mary adulation had more to do with a collective mother fixation—indeed, more anxiety than philosophy. She claimed Marian visions were driven by unconscious yearnings for a return to the early goddess cults. I responded dismissively. She laughed—yes, men in general were misinformed and this accounted for my attitude.

"Yeah, well, I least I'm not violent," I said, "not yet anyway," faking some anxious twitch and widening my eyes Peter Lorie -style.

"That's not funny," she said.

The Virgin Mary statue at the Cathedral of St. John

of God had been weeping real tears—it was in the papers—and apparently it could solve people's problems if they invested enough money or prayer in it. But the tears dried up over time and recently an angry patron had gone and shot the thing. Sophie wanted to see the bullet holes before it became another kind of pilgrimage site. When we got there, though, the place was empty—empty and vast—a disused Catholic cathedral in a Southside gray zone. The bullet holes had been filled with plaster and, indeed, there were no tears running down Our Lady's inanimate cheeks anymore. In fact, the Virgin looked away as we talked about her, as if ashamed of the controversy.

"She seems so meek," I said. "It's hard to believe anyone could be threatened."

"If she wasn't a threat why did they shoot her?"

"They?"

"Not *they*, that guy, you know. The guy who shot her. Him. The dude."

"He shot her cause she stopped. Or maybe it was a typically Chicago reaction to the introduction of grace, it could only foster one response—a gun. "Besides," I went on, "people shoot anything these days, coke machines, statues of Elvis, their wives, their children, the president, Andy Warhol. Everyone is angry and there's no other way to express it, apparently."

She said, "Jokes. Sex. These are also expressions. And, no one dies."

I said "People don't get jokes and sex mostly makes them mad."

She laughed. I sneered. Some low-level cleric gave us the eye so we split. Besides it wasn't a commercially viable neighborhood and dusk was upon us. We agreed on the general desperation of the faithful and the odd disguises desire and denial must take. Furthermore, we appeared to have accepted own moral message of healing and forgiveness, which is about all you can really ask of a church visit.

There was, after all, in our own lives a certain amount of healing to be done. The whole Arnaud affair had people on edge. A lot of us couldn't come to grips with what might have caused it. Arnaud claimed it was violent sex play—that Stacey had wanted to be strangled during her orgasm, and when she did climax, it went on too long and she died. Arnaud told the police he did not realize what was happening—she acted so ecstatic. This was hard to swallow because Stacey didn't seem like a "please strangle me," type. Though Arnaud did seem like an obliger. Still, there must have been a moment when the possibility of her death occurred to him and he went ahead and strangled her anyway.

Should he be forgiven? Was he guilty until proven innocent? We believed ourselves empathetic to the need to experience extremes, but not if we had to answer for the consequences. In any case, Arnaud's transcendental sex story would do him no good in court, so the lawyer was going to use insanity as a defense—it was the trend of the times. Arnaud had apparently also been telling the lawyer a lot of way-out stories as background justification. There was, for instance, some long-ago cult association and a charismatic Manson-like guru who had convinced Arnaud that this world was but a vale of tears and that only sex or death, or a combination thereof, could truly break through.

"He needed a guru for that?" I laughed, but I took the laugh back under the critical gaze of my companions.

And there were other problems. The lawyer needed friends to testify that Arnaud was in effect, bonkers, so they were summoning some of these so-called friends to a pre-trial inquest. Kathe had some experience in this—she casually admitted to having had a boyfriend once who was also accused of murder. This was news to everyone. It was hard to place her in the "women who love men who kill" category. Still, having access to lawyers and legal information, she started advising Boggs long distance. This reopened the door to Bernadette's confidence, and within a few weeks everything was patched up between them.

With the gradual re-acceptance of Kathe, it became safe for Sophie to move from Ravenswood to the eastside, and into my building: monthly rent, no lease, a sitcom bohemia, and the El train ran by the rear windows, adding appropriately noir accents. Indeed, the subtle, periodic shaking of the building was often mistaken for an underlying unfocused passion in the neighborhood—exactly what had attracted lonely single renters like myself.

Even though we virtually lived together, Sophie and I managed to keep our relationship private. We often appeared in public and argued as only a couple could, but most people figured we were entirely unsuited for each other and that we must be "just friends." When the news finally did break, it met with general disapproval. Some said it was the scandal we loved, not each other. Some said it was based on our mutually misguided romantic outlooks and that our tryst would collapse within a month. Others thought it was merely the classic attraction between beauty and ugliness, vitality and apathy. Apparently I was the latter example in each case. One guy said "You shouldn't sleep with your friends," but we had never really been friends, so he was off the mark on that.

*

Looking back, I could list her attractions: the pale, slow curve of her shoulder, the ungainliness of carriage, the lightning quick changes her mouth and eyes could work, her enduring obsession with last year's fashions. I also thought the dark-rimmed glasses were sexy. She looked different depending on the slant of the frames—cute, intelligent, helpless, even dorky. But what most fascinated me was the elliptical nature of her mind—the way it could traverse whole fields of ideas, moving like a fast-tracking camera from the utterly absurd to the naively profound, from the clichéd to the uncommon. It kept me off-balance and I liked that at the time.

One day Bernadette threw a magazine on the coffee table with an "ah-ha" sneer. *Newsweek* was claiming that sociologists were claiming that biologists were claiming that there is no real love in the world and that humans were primarily attracted to symmetry and consistency. There were ratios of hip to waist to breast to shoulder—4 to 1, 3 to 2—I don't remember. Whatever it was, love could apparently be broken down to numbers, making the beauty of the body—like a gothic cathedral or a well-constructed symphony—a mere manifestation of mathematical progressions, especially as it moved and the numbers rubbed against each other. Chemicals were part of it, too, pheromones they called them—oxytocin, estrogen—olfactory cowboys and cowgirls riding from one body to another, binding them on a molecular, instinctual level.

But there were opposing arguments. Psychologists proposed narcissism; many people, after all, marry someone who looks just like them. Marxists supposed it was the economic exploitation of the emanated, fetishized self. More optimistic cultural critics, advertisers to be exact, believed we all have a hidden shining inner self that can be brought out with the right shampoo, handbag or other accessory. And then there were darker theories—that we are looking for some kind of punishment in love, working out great primordial formulas of loss and anger. This pessimistic analysis appealed to me, especially in light of how most relationships turn out.

"There's no magic," Berny said. "It just makes sense."

"But 'sense' itself doesn't make sense, unless you define it as such," I said, feeling clever.

Berny turned it around: "Well, nonsense is sense too, if you think about it. It's all a matter of framing." She went on to cite her dead mentor St. Bernard, in whose view, she claimed, the spiritual and the physical were not fundamentally different. Then as now—materialism is the law. The spirit, gods, even self—these are affects of matter.

I countered, saying that was hardly an apropos statement from one who claimed kinship with the accused 12th-century advocate of *"fin amour."* Secondly, "materialism," as it is practiced in our times, was merely a style, and the style would change once people realized that, carried to an extreme, they lost their free will in the worship of it. I mean—if you know everything, you know how things will turn out, and that's no fun, so we avoid knowledge in favor of entertainment.

But Sophie said what makes something entertaining is the fact that you do know how it will turn out in the general sense.

Bernadette reiterated the *Newsweek* premise: it's all a sequence of hidden switches in our DNA, and it doesn't matter how we interpret things.

"So materialism and mysticism are sympathetic?" I asked.

"Exactly," she said, thinking she had tricked me into supporting her argument.

I went on to claim that the bond between Sophie and I was to be found in a likeness of mind, *not* in crude physical triggers. Berny said it could all be boiled down to exchange value. I was hurt—truth is I refused to think of myself as being without will or emotional agency, a mere shopper. There were too many forces at play—narrative longing for one. Sophia Walker/Wagner and I could be part of a genre. We both believed in the possibility of objects and people as spiritual doorways. At least I pretended to. We both believed in a certain sanctity of chance. Berny called those beliefs nothing if not non-committal.

In sum, it was a ridiculous conversation. We were pretentious, and apparently we didn't care. We did, however, feel a need to make this pretension bear on the situations of our friends, and so the talk returned to the subject of our little personal murder show:

Did Arnaud kill Stacey because he could no longer tolerate her beauty or her affection? Did Stacey have a death wish? Maybe Arnaud achieved climax at the same moment as his partner and lost control for that reason. What about suppressed anger? Did Stacey deny his independence and thus cause his rebellion?

Was the whole thing a little "Paradise Lost" acted out in the garden of a Cuyler Street apartment? Did anybody care other than the police? And what sort of obsession drove the police to take those jobs as guardians of the state, anyway? And how did that issue inform our discussion? Maybe it was a suicide pact after all.

"I think he was high," Bernadette said. "He *was* doing a lot of meth."

I hadn't heard that before. I don't know how he would have afforded the drugs because he never had a job.

*

In those days none of us had real jobs. It was all contingency work. I was writing freelance catalogue copy about plastic disco shoes made in Atlanta. Sophie was a freelance window dresser's assistant at Fields. Kathe had an temporary ad-house job, and her new boyfriend worked as an on-call oyster shucker at Nick's downtown. Some people were starting to get what was called computer work. No one really knew what that entailed, and part of the job, apparently, was figuring it out. Mostly we went to clubs and parties where people who looked a lot like us argued over issues we were supposed to be interested in—over bands and art, poetry and books, and computers.

It was the 80s and imagined conflict was the trend. Mac and IBM might have been football teams for all the passionate rivalry they spawned. Neo-Expressionists were pitting themselves against the Avant-Imagists, whom they considered to be Old School. The Flamboyant Super Realists hated everybody, especially the Latter-Day Surrealists. Then there were the Muscular Expressionists and the Neo Pre-Rafaelites. Each aesthetic label had a uniform. Some wore sharkskin; others wore chinos. I knew guys who designed paint-splattered t-shirts to wear to the clubs.

There was, as well, a general ennui, due to the feeling that everything had already been done. This made the world seem old. But the world *was* old—that's what really bothered everyone. But then we needed it to be old; it helped in our search for authenticity, a concept or quality that many believed didn't exist anyway. This gave birth to the "call your bluff syndrome," so labeled by Bernadette, whereby everybody tried to out everybody else as a poseur.

"Oh, he's really from the suburbs," they would say, or "He's not an artist, he just went to art school."

Another common argument centered on "selling out." It was never really clear exactly when that happened—when the sale took place, or what was sold, or to whom. Some believed that selling out simply meant freedom from self-inflicted poverty. Many people were on both sides of that fence and found it difficult to take a stand without embarrassment. Bernadette claimed it was all one great fiasco and that the thing to do was to stand back and enjoy it. Capitalism appropriated its enemies and made us all playmates. No one knew what was good or bad. Before it arrived they wanted it. After it arrived they hated it. Secretly, they loved it. But no one loved it enough to ever admit it. You might or might not be invited to certain events depending on whether you owned up to your ambition or not. If you didn't, you were either "too pure" and thus laughable, or a liar. Maybe shooting the Virgin Mary or murdering one's spouse was simply a way out—no more decisions to make, no more acting—just three hots and a cot and plenty of time to write your memoirs.

*

As for Sophie and I, we pursued a life of surreal *errance* in those days, wandering through the thrift shops and used bookstores of the city. We'd meet for drinks in antique lounges where the cocktails were served on napkins with old printed cartoon jokes. We held rendezvous in the city's conservatories—those recesses of luxury and lost sensuality. We made an adventure out of the old baroque theaters of the Loop—The State-Lake, the Woods, the Oriental—watching a bit of one movie here, part of another there. One day we combined an old vampire film with a movie about an orchid keeper who goes insane, puts his wife in a blender and feeds her to his plants. Afterwards, over happy-hour oysters at the Berghoff, we discussed cannibalism, transcendence, pedophilia, Dracula and Lolita. We agreed the exchange of body fluids was a dangerous event no matter when it took place. You don't know what to expect—a passionate kiss or the sinking of passionate fangs into your passionate neck.

"No love can measure up to death or insanity," I said.

"That's exactly what you *would* say," she said, thinking she knew me that well.

The Loop *was* somehow an old movie to us, and being there was our way of circumscribing our lives within a set. It was Bernadette who insisted we go to the opera with her, in that the suspension of disbelief required was liberating. Sophie didn't know if she liked opera. She did like new wave, punk and Motown. Piaf and Patsy made her cry. But she cried easily anyway.

One night *Pandora's Box* was playing at the Music Box. The showing was timed to coincide with Berg's *Lulu*, which was up at the Lyric. The four of us went to both. After all, *Lulu* was the only serial killer opera we knew of, which alone was enough to pique Sophie's interest. I was more interested in the other killers, the audience themselves—the bad cologne trapped in the fur of the skinned animals they wore for status, as if the migration of life toward our human hierarchy led naturally to their fate as adornment. But then I was wearing a black leather jacket, so I was no different. Besides the high-pitched screaming onstage matched my mental picture of Arnaud and Stacey in their coital suicide attempt. The world is a wiggle picture, move it just slightly one way or the other and the grandiose act becomes despotic, ecstasy becomes death. *Lulu* ended with a giant cage coming up out of the ground, trapping the heroine's soul. That part, at least, seemed true.

We left the theater in a state of ambivalence. If the singing hurt, I did enjoy the production values. But that's what you pay the money for—production—that big cage coming up out of the ground, the fantastic lights.

That night Sophie and I got into some kind of fight, produced, I suppose, out of the momentum of our theatrical experience, and the idea of women as willing victims. It began by her asking if I had ever hit a woman, and if I ever would. This, she posed as a kind of joke, but it quickly turned serious, with her remembering various instances when she was sure I wanted to hit her: "I bet you want to sometimes."

I denied it.

But it seemed like she was daring me. "You probably couldn't even do it." She said I wasn't man enough, too introverted, or something to that effect. She was laughing but the laughter was a lie.

I said I wouldn't be baited like her other boyfriends.

She got a little mad. "What other boyfriends?"

"I don't know," I said, "You're the one that tells me this stuff. It seems to me sometimes you get men to treat you bad on purpose, like it's a test or something."

"Oh, now I'm like Stacey—I get a thrill out of abuse. Is that what you're saying?"

"I didn't start this conversation."

She called me an asshole. It was an odd turn in the relationship, but, after all, aggression and surrender can be the same, especially in sex. And so we went to bed, shaken but resolved to do the deed.

*

After the sex, we went to sleep and I had a dream. I saw a cloud the color of fire, and in the cloud, a woman, frightening and yet somehow filled with a marvelous joy. In her arms she held a baby wrapped in crimson cloth. I felt it was the child Sophie had once been. In one hand the lordly woman held a fiery object. What it was I could not tell. She said, *"vide cor tuum."* Then, of course, I knew.

The woman then woke the sleeping child and made her eat the glowing object. And the child who was Sophie did so, ravenously. Then the woman turned to me and said, "*Dei tuoi figli la madre tu vedi vinta e afflitta, fatta trista per te, e pur d ate proscritta.*" I thought this meant "Are you hungry, Frank?" But then, a few moments later, with an air of sadness, the two of them ascended to heaven, or some other place I was not invited.

*

I woke up and took a cold ginger ale out of the fridge. I went to the window and stared in the direction of the lake. It was dark and the web of streetlights was flickering due to some flaw in the ten thousand thousand relay switches of the wiring of the city, and I wondered if there was any decision I had made in my life that I had really made.

(four)

Sophie gleaned where others labored to decipher. She learned through images that coalesced in her mind about tendencies that in turn swirled around intentions disguised as choices. As far as morality went, Sophie pronounced upon such questions without reference to textual or historical example.

In relation to Arnaud such questions came up continually: Why would he want to kill Stacey? Was he a victim of some fad for perverse crime? Was it violent television that drove him to this vile act? Or was it the tattoos that dictated the killing? Did the images move from his skin to his mind, redirecting the neural electricity down differing, even more violent, pathways? And if that was so, did exposure to those images also imprint *our* behavior? Was society a projection of the psyche? Or vice versa? Or did we all simply live in a hall of mirrors of infinite selves, a hall of obsessive biologically-driven consumption?

It was Bernadette's contention that consumer society, in fact, *depended* on the destabilization of the personality. This instability kept everyone shopping, working toward meaningless goals—plaques on the mantel, awards in trade magazines, things like that. Advertising was nothing but the onslaught of the impossible, an endless invitation to dissatisfaction. It was a wonder anyone managed to stay intact, much less moral, under such circumstances. For Berny, this fragmentation was an assault on self-coherence. For Sophie it was a profound creative force, which she felt free to exploit. In fact, she often claimed, as a joke, to be a kind of royalty, a Queen of Multiple Personalities, a claim that aroused no particular concern in those days—after all, we're talking about a crowd of pseudo-schizophrenics here. Maybe it was a contest. But Sophie was actually good at the role—she could change her personality right in front of you and never give it a second thought. She considered it a social skill. I'd seen her switch her position on a topic in mid-conversation without being remotely aware or caring. She could back-pedal on a dime, and do so with the moral facility of a sitcom character or a modern-day politician.

If I failed to engage in this endless dialectic, Sophie would attribute the apathy to my supposed habit of never taking her seriously. And so I eventually did learn to argue according to her demands, but I blamed my attitudes on her desire—her needs, not mine. I thought myself more consistent. Berny said that I just needed entertainment.

It was, indeed, amusing to watch Sophie's face slide effortlessly from irony to laughter to anger, all within the same subject matter. Her color too wavered, along with her convictions, from a flushed erotic red, to a jaundiced yellow, to a mystic pale. She could exhibit in the same second a triumphal air of dominion *and* a primal sense of injustice, of having been cheated by life, changes that flickered like the firelight of vanity on a wall in her personal Platonic cave. Her blue eyes could darken to the color of thunder or a tormented romantic seascape. Her well of rage was frightening, deep, seismic and violent, and she could tap it as needed. She could steal the poison of your own words and turn it on you. It was also clear that she disliked this aspect of herself, as she often collapsed after such acts into apologetic submission.

I sometimes wondered if this changeability was physical, as it did seem to be rooted in mechanical processes. Or, perhaps I was merely mistaking the effect for the cause, a popular form of intellectual laziness with much historical precedence. It is often thought that saints and other visionaries were actually experiencing some kind of temporal lobe seizures, and Sophie was quick to draw this connection between beatitude and her own so variable condition. That was too blatant for me, although I did agree that most religion is a matter of nerves. In any case, her fascination with female chemistry, emotional extremism, and religious imagery made "The Callas Project" seem like the inevitably perfect endeavor.

*

Bernadette enlisted Sophie in this new art project and they started to put together plans for the installation, which they would do at Gilles' and Solomon's thrift shop. Berny claimed they would be putting that space to good use since they obviously weren't selling anything anyway. The first thing Berny did was put two pictures in the window: one was Callas in Paris look-ing out her window on the Boulevard Georges Man-del; the other was the Kumari Devi, the Living God-dess of Kathmandu looking out her window onto the Hanumandhoka Palace Square. Both photos depicted a woman, or girl, looking out a window on a balcony, holding a curtain aside. What was significant was the relationship between idolization and abandonment. And then there was the extreme sexlessness that both women were condemned to, a neutering meant to meet the respective demands of divinity.

Gilles put a sign in the window: "Coming Soon, 'The Kallas Project.'" This title, including the intention-al misspelling, eventually became the unofficial name of the store, since the store never actually had a name.

"The Kallas Project" evolved out of something Ber-ny had been thinking of doing earlier, an installation piece which involved blow-ups of photos of the faces of various singers of iconographic stature—Holiday, Piaf, Joplin, etc.—fragmented in a manner that was meant to demonstrate a relationship between the laws of symme-try and the laws of morality. A patch of skin from each face would be enlarged to show the pores, the cells, the grain. This divide-and-magnify technique would con-tinue all the way to the molecular level, and deeper. It was never determined how exactly Berny would ac-complish this display, being without any technological means. We just took it for granted that it was, in fact, possible.

Sophie came up with the idea of using tape loops of

voices, which would be gradually slowed down or sped up. The tape would function as an aural corollary to the disintegrating photograph. They would collaborate on a text, the idea being to describe each voice in terms of palate and aftertaste, like a wine critic might, but the words, appearing on video screens, would also disintegrate, or rather, be reduced and reproduced as binary strings of digits.

"The Project" continued to mutate. Eventually, due to evident time constraints, the other singers were dropped and it was simply Callas. Bernadette wanted to have a little doll of the famous soprano turning on a spindle, but that idea changed to a film of a Kerala Kathakali dancer projected at varying speeds and over-dubbed with an operatic soundtrack. At various stages there was a glass pyramid, a labyrinth, and a chess-board involved.

One afternoon they were sitting around the store running through some permutations of "The Project," when some errant but concerned customer overheard and criticized them for their advocacy of such a clichéd and bourgeois figure.

"C'mon," he said," she's a little overdone, don't you think. Who cares about her anymore?"

Bernadette countered that she didn't really care what anybody thought, besides clichés came into existence for a reason—the point being to expose the hidden architecture of human meaning. "Music frozen in time" was a cliché about architecture, but what about architecture dissolved into music. Bernadette reminded us that Callas' mouth had once been described as a gothic cathedral, thus merging the architectural, the religious and the sonic in one image.

We then began to speculate with the customer as to which gothic cathedral the mouth of Maria Callas might best be compared. Notre Dame was too touristy. Kathe volunteered the idea of Chartres, what with its subterranean Black Virgin, but it was also touristy. I suggested St. Sulpice might coincide with the woman's semi-demonic character, but St. Sulpice was not gothic, and Chartres was just as demonic. The customer who had started the discussion left, no doubt disappointed by our irreverence. Or maybe it was the pungent clouds of pot smoke that scared him off. We barely noticed.

By the end of the afternoon we had settled on the idea, not of a cathedral, but of a miniature golf course. This was Sophie's idea—an entire miniature golf course composed of opera singers' heads. Each head would be the size of a small tool shed. You knocked in the ball and an aria played while the singer's eyes opened and closed like a giant iron clown. This then became the focus of a whole new art project, which would require funding. We got out pencils and pads of paper. We wrote down the names of nine singers and nine songs, then a list of supplies: papier-mâché, chicken wire. We drew maps. It took up about two hours and by the end we were absolutely sure we were going to do it. We'd get financial backing somehow—maybe an Arts Council grant. The room grew heavy with the weight of liberal arts educations hanging like albatrosses around our necks.

*

I don't remember exactly how the Virgin Mary crept into the plan. It was the weekend of Bernadette's B-movie marathon, another of her big ideas—forty-eight hours of Bergman, Bertolucci, Bunuel and Brooks. This also would be held at the store—beginning Friday at 7pm. People could drop by, before and after work, after the bars closed, when they got up in the morning, mix and match as they chose, drink, eat. And of course we would record everything everyone said, maybe write a play or a film script based on the conversations.

Somewhere along on Saturday afternoon *That Obscure Object of Desire* was playing. We laughed at the sad antics of Fernando Rey. Sophie accused me of retroactively appropriating his character and thereby casting her in the "object of desire" role, which she disapproved of. I said I never did such a thing, or if I did, I was merely trying to know her, which meant having to define her. "Exactly," she said. To be known like that was her privilege, but my crime. Then someone said the original object of desire was the Virgin Mary—and the cult of wanting what you can't have.

Sophie said, "Frank has a Mary obsession," referring to some religious books I had.

"Actually, that's your obsession, not mine."

"Are you sure?" she asked. And because she asked, I wasn't sure. I did know Sophie was adamantly anti-maternal—in those days, most women under thirty were—but that didn't make her Marian.

*

Things were changing subtly. It was hard to put my finger on why. Sophie became a victim of her own *fin de siècle* malaise. It bothered me, but it added to her appeal—this false victimhood. But it also made her angry. By extension, her sharp tongue could be seen as a defense against those dilettantes and poseurs who might try to trap her in submissive roles. At least that's how she saw it. Certainly she had a liquid wit, often witheringly acidic, and an ability to level someone with a seemingly off-handed remark. Men were hopelessly attracted. Women bent both ways. She was a study for Bernadette, who was no slouch herself when it came to withering opinions.

As for me, all that wit was mildly entertaining, until it was used against me. Indeed, I started to notice the slow increase in off-handed comments directed my way. Sophie herself claimed to have little control: "I didn't mean anything by that," she would say, as if her tongue preceded her like a car driven by a drunk, that, if it happened to hit you, well, you probably you deserved it. "Oh I don't know how that slipped out, you must have wanted me to say that," she would say. Or my favorite: "I don't know, it sounded good when I said it." Beauty begged forgiveness, but there were limits.

The idea of psycho-biography as art was just becoming prominent. The competition of the marketplace was infecting the law of the bedroom with a Machevellian sense of intimacy in which every gesture, every touch was overloaded with agenda. Hyper-attuned to the least negative nuance of tone, we began to circle each other, vibrating with paranoia and insecurity. I had my unsupportable sense of entitlement. She had her birthright, which she felt was absolute. I saw her artistic pretensions as an insult to the working class. She saw my attraction to bohemian life as a pose, a rejection of responsibility. The same was true with my distaste for confrontation. I blamed my parents. She blamed me.

She saw as negative what I saw as positive. I said she invited aggression; "I think you want to be punished," was a favorite phrase I often used against her. She said she wanted me to think that. I said her ruse of testing my character was really an excuse for weakness. But she called it a survival skill, learned the hard way. We came to hate each other's friends for no real reason. She hated critical company, which I thought was odd, being as she was the most critical person I knew. Bernadette was an exception in Sophie's normal entourage, which was mostly people who were easily impressed by her. But she claimed that it was I who chose my friends on the basis of flattery—to bolster my ego, which was weak, like my will.

Our romance grew increasingly fragile as we tore into each other's flaws, but we blamed it on modern life, and we found and read the books that told us we were right to do so. It was Kathe who said that the new intimate terrorism was not so much a trend as a liberating perspective. People had been far too slaphappy and it was time to get serious and realize love was not a good thing, but rather a mode of oppression enforced by outdated romantic ideals, which were never more than ways of maintaining the male-dominated financial and social hegemony. I hated the word hegemony, but there it was, a mark of my own fall into triviality and one-up-man-ship.

Bernadette and Kathe sat back and laughed. They smoked their cigarettes and took a vicarious thrill in watching the decay of the romantic universe working itself out before their eyes. They would say things like Act Three, Scene Two, whenever Sophie and I began to argue in public. We were glad to provide them with the theater by which to rekindle their friendship, but the consequences were bad all around. Sophie drew away from Bernadette. "The Kallas Project" fell apart. Before I knew it, she and Berny were outright enemies and I was caught in the middle. Bernadette started blaming Sophie for Kathe's alienation. She said I would have been better off with Kathe. Sophie claimed Bernadette had returned to Kathe because she, Sophie, was too independent and Bernadette couldn't manipulate her.

The whole thing was getting so complicated I decided to stay home, at least mentally. There was a TV show in my head that I wanted to watch. I'd get a six-pack and some chips and settle down on the couch in my secret rec-room. The walls were Wellwood-paneled and the mini-fridge was always stocked. I could be at some public event among false and hostile friends and not have a clue.

What I didn't understand at the time was that Sophie was a harbinger. Yes, eventually everyone I knew would resemble her. And I would perpetually be a victim of their unrequited drama—loved for my role, but hated for playing it. Sophie attacked me on grounds of complicity. If I acquiesced, she shot me down for being what I thought she wanted me to be. She baited me into situations, then accused me of being there by my own scheming. It changed day by day—every *coup de theatre*, every barbed comment, every significant absence—everything was a pre-emptive strike on her part, causing me to more and more exhibit the very behaviors she accused me of. And if she was going to accuse me of violent tendencies, my defense was always: I would not have thought of them otherwise.

I've always wondered what it is that makes someone strike out or refrain—what force is at play at that infinitesimal pivotal moment when one either gives in to the rage or not. That's not to say I ever wanted to hit her, but I've known plenty of guys who would have. I just laughed, as if the laughter could replace the impulse, or vent it. Sophie tried to control my reaction: "He's laughing at himself," I could hear her thinking. I was sure that she also assumed I was belittling her. Many nights we lay next to each other embarrassed and depleted.

We actually went to a relationship counselor—one Betty Somebody. We got a good rate because Betty was Sophie's friend. Still, our sessions amounted to little more than: "I'm not your mother"; "Yeah, well I'm not your father either." Not exactly Shakespearean discourse. I claimed inherent bias. I thought that we were being manipulated by Ms. Betty Somebody for cash and career-validation. The process felt like going to a car mechanic in the age of planned obsolescence; there's nothing he or she can do but put in used parts, tell you they're new and take as much money as possible. And so, on Betty Somebody's, recommendation, we went to another shrink for a couple of hours, but that one didn't want to have anything to do with us. My fault again, apparently. The funny thing was, we could always stop at some point and laugh about our situation; somehow our sense of absurdity helped us into the next day. But the thing about laughter is—it's a pinnacle; you can slide down either side anytime.

*

One day Sophie found a box of old Victorian-style greeting cards at Amvets and she bought them because it matched the color scheme of her apartment with the chenille bedspreads and the melon-color paint. We hung out there often; we loved the bitter enigma, the perfume of regret, the sublime banality of the afternoon and we often sought its dark heart, its metaphorical Kurtz in the jungle of emotion. In fact, I often heard Marlon Brando's voice distinctly whispering, "the Melancholy, the Melancholy" in our ears as we lay about, drinking gin and tonics and watching the trains go by, while the wind animated the empty clothes on the laundry lines. It's prophetic in a way, how the subtle train of thought-events can move you forward.

But back to the box of cards: since Berny had once suggested we all go on a field trip to Calcutta, to the temple of Kali, it was only normal that Sophie would find in all this ephemeral distraction a hidden directive to go to Paris instead. Kali=Temple=Cathedral=Medieval=gothic=Paris. It was a complicated way of arriving at a decision, and the truth is it could have easily had as much to do with the correspondences between the color schemes of her Victorian greeting card collection and our desire for a rose-tinted future. I really believe the world works that way—less as will and more as subtle suggestion.

*

Sophie was big on nicknames and sometimes called me Richard Speck because she saw a resemblance. And so in revenge I tried to come up with an equivalent nickname for her, but I never found one I liked. I did try "Simone" for awhile, as in Collinet/de Beauvoir. It didn't matter. Sophie thought I was attacking her pretensions, but it had more to do with our recently revived interest in surrealist lifestyles and existential malaise.

Imagine a Simone de Beauvoir wanna-be and a Richard Speck look-alike on an operating room table under the gaze of a roomful of students studying the mating habits of irreconcilable archetypes. It's not that strange because—that's how sex usually was with us. We always felt as if someone was watching us, expecting something interesting to happen. It's a drag to make up scenarios that oppress you, but it happens all the time. You read something about the guard dogs at the gates of hell or paradise and it gets in your head, literally.

One night we were drinking at a new bar in the South Loop—the *Bar des Oiseaux*. It was a theme bar for art students from the Institute and Columbia. There were pictures of Andre Breton and Robert Desnos on the wall. At the end of the evening, we took the Howard home. When we got to our building, a rabid dog stood growling at us before the entrance. One of the neighbors fired a gun into the air and scared the dog away. I said "Thanks man." "No problemo," the guy replied. He was drunk and the gun in his hand was wobbly like a Salvador Dali Spanish rifle made of jelly. "I should have killed the bitch. But then I'd get in trouble," he said, looking to the ground. Puccini's "Pagliacci" was playing softly from somebody's window: *"Ridi, Pagliacchio, sul tuo amore infranto! Ridi del duol che t'avvelena il cor!"*

Sophie and I got in an argument as soon as the door shut—something about hand guns, stray dogs, and the romance of alienation. We just couldn't help ourselves. Eventually the neighbors couldn't stand the shouting anymore and the landlord asked us to leave. Any other couple would have thrown punches, had revenge sex, or taken classes at the Learning Annex, but we decided on the slightly more expensive alternative of going away together on a foreign adventure. We would have a *real* experience even if it killed us. This was no doubt part of what led to our downfall—a kind of Bovaryism of the collective psyche. We actually didn't want real experience because real life is boring and everyone knows it. But there we were, smack in the middle of it.

Actually we didn't know where we were, or what the middle was. Sensation is temporary. Brahma blinks his eyes—the universes come and go. People get hurt. Marriages break apart. Kali and Shiva copulate and the world shakes like golden foil. There's only so much you can attribute to the great spiritual wheel—the rest is blight and sadness of the flesh. So do what the TV tells you to do—pretend there's a world out there waiting for you. I read an ad somewhere, maybe in the *New Yorker*, maybe *Newsweek*. It said "Be Yourself. Get Away." As it happened Betty Somebody had a friend who was a travel agent. Coincidence? Maybe. Or maybe it was a scent, a surreal smoke trail that we followed from the 44th Ward to Islington, to the fetishized streets of the 18th Arrondisement, to the Colaba district in Bombay and finally to the Kalighat of Calcutta, city of Kali Ma in romantic Bengal.

Part Two

(five)

The juice of experience is best tasted from its blossom. Ramakrishna would kiss and suck the flowers of Kali's feet. He would swim in the sweat of her terrifying thigh, kissing the flower opening within Kali's vagina. The saint became a fish within the ocean of the Goddess body, loving each blossom as it appeared: the anus first, then the labia, followed by the navel, then the incredible complexity of Kali's twelve-petaled heart. He made love to her heart with his tongue till her heart burst. He made love to the lotus of her throat until it too burst. Upon arriving at that place where the spine meets the skull, he made love to it as well until the sublime light escaped the head and the climactic thousand-petaled lotus of the universe was realized.

London and Paris came and went, not without incident. Looking back on things, however, sometimes the show seemed so highly edited, so purposely manipulated to a certain effect, that we could have just rented the video. In fact, Sophie would sometimes claim the whole trip was not only extremely "video-like," but a supreme directorial effort on my part to present a particular version of reality, one that would put her on shaky ground, after which I could turn and offer myself as guardian and protector. But I was no guide. I was my own Goodman Brown in this forest of symbol and bliss. The allusion may seem absurd but it goes some substantial way in explaining how Sophie and I ended up in Bombay, a city shaped like the can-opener on a Swiss Army Knife poised to open a tin can of condensed milk.

*

The ride from the airport into Bombay proper is a monumental confrontation with poverty that stretches on and on like multiplying football fields of colored rags hung out to dry alongside shacks made of rusted sheet steel and old shower curtains—whole neighborhoods following the same decorative scheme were stretched out adjacent to dubious construction sites where women carried baskets of hand-broken stone on their heads, with babies in one arm and brass bowls of water in the other. Starving crowds clawed at the bus as it barreled in fits and starts, grinding through the low gears slowly in the monstrous traffic.

A tout found us a room at the Sea Foam Hotel, so-named because of the view of the sea and its dirty foam. Outside our window, across the street, at a skyscraper construction site, skinny guys in turbans were walking barefoot on bamboo scaffolds, holding pots of liquid concrete on their heads, rolling wheel-barrows of steaming tar over cane catwalks and driving nails into floor joists with bricks. There were pictures of the Taj Mahal in the hotel hallway. Sophie said, "Hey look Frank, the Taj." Sophie loved the Taj, she loved the whole idea of it. "Love is the last adventure," she used to say. The Taj Hotel was just down the road. The stores inside the Taj were expensive and air-conditioned and one could atrophy in the lobby for hours, even as the monster city smoldered out there, crying in pain.

In the city of Mumbadevi even the rats look sick and the children follow you for miles because they have no homes. There is little to distract the stranger from the misery, or the beauty for that matter, as they are strangely the same. People tried to pick us up. Sophie's blondeness, her overtly confident carriage, attracted all kinds of "tour guides" who could show her just about anything in the city, or the country, or even those no less real destinations in her mind. These guides had homemade pamphlets with awkwardly written introductions to wonderful adventures. They knew secret parts of town. They had exclusive access. They wanted to be near us, so much so that Sophie said she often felt their hands lightly touching her hair as if it were a western halo.

Poverty, combined with rampant development and the lack of safety standards, left many people crippled or otherwise maimed, and the odd configurations of crutches and jerry-rigged limbs could be read like a script, some weird cryptic alphabet of absence, a language of want being written before our eyes in the moving bodies of suffering citizens. The great heads of the hydrocephalic children seemed like containers of unexpressed dreams. The dead and the extremely thin, the deflated skin bags in the gutters—these were signs of the spiritual food chain of which we were mere links. It really was like a dream and, after all, we were shopping for these things, these dreams, and since we shopped, we arrogantly believed we deserved what we shopped for. So after we settled in we went out to what some brochure said was a great little restaurant where the biryani was to die for.

I tried to sleep that night but I wasn't tired. I couldn't concentrate either because of the sounds that carried across the wide flat sky—the prayers, the cries of the vultures circling the Pharisee Temples of Silence, even the prophetic howling of the young whores of far-off Falkland Road. The Penguin Veda we'd brought with us was laying open, turned down on the bed. I picked it up, sat down and read a passage: "*The child of waters is self-engendered,*" it claimed, "*The child of waters never fades, he shines forever with undarkened flames.*" I dozed off but woke again sometime later, thinking about the freelance dentists waiting for us out on the street. They would pull our teeth for a dollar, and they would wait forever to do it, too. Sooner or later we would be old. It's hard to escape the assault of symbols.

*

A week passed, maybe more, and somehow we found ourselves on a mail train from Mangalore to Mysore. It took two days to go a hundred miles. People walked alongside the train and held long philosophical conversations with the passengers. We were sick and sun-stroked when we arrived in Mysore. Besides the famous Mysore yoga center, there was a local leprosy clinic, which spilled its patients into the streets like animated flesh blossoms. This "human flower" metaphor, I thought, might account for the rumors of sexual promiscuity amongst leper colonies—petals, pistils, cocks and cunts. But Sophie said that promiscuous sex might just be an attempt to feel more, and, in fact, that's why everyone indulges in sex—perhaps as the last refuge of physical certainty in a sensationally overloaded world. But this sounded like sensory sentimentalism to me.

Coincidentally, we were interrupted by one of these flower women, begging for food at some cathedral door frequented by tourists. This brought us back to the real world where, apparently, the disintegration of the body was more painful than mystical. The subject of pain then led us to an argument about some of Sophie's friends. Apparently I had a long-standing grudge against one "Doris," a secretary with a persecution complex. I couldn't identify with Doris's pain and I had said as much one night during another argument about the causes of hysteria. This opened the door to other wrong-doings on my part. For instance, there was also a "Margaret," whom I had, apparently, called a lout and an overeater. Sophie said she agreed, but only in principle. Then she laughed. Then she claimed it was I who lacked empathy and not her. I denied this. We finally dropped this subject. The leper lady had long since moved away. We spent the rest of the week walking up and down the shores of Kukarahalli Lake getting all transcendental and romantic.

*

The next stop in our travelogue was Puri, home town of Jagannatha—yet another Lord of the Universe and the final benign incarnation of Vishnu before the world falls back into bellicosity and chaos. There is, in Puri, a ten-acre platform shaped like a sea shell, and there stands a monumental temple where wooden dolls of Lord Jagannatha are fed popcorn, coconut candy, bananas and curd. Once a year at the Yatha Ratha, the Juggernaut, mad devotees carry Jagannathas through the streets in cars shaped like upturned bra cups. It is said Jagannatha is like a particle *and* a Sacred Log of Wood, but he is also an erotic child.

I have a theory that most religions are inherently pedophilic, and the cult of Jagannatha bears this out. Jagannatha looks like a two year old with a pierced nose and he has no hands or feet to resist the lecherous advances of the rapacious religious mind. And yet Jagannatha dharma is neither intellectual conformity nor ceremonial piety. Indeed, he is expansive and constrictive, pluralistic and sectarian; he is not an amalgam but a synthesis. I read all this in a pamplet on the Bala Danda, a plaza full of image vendors. I bought the smallest image I could find to keep in my pocket for luck. Sophie had the idea that Jagannatha was probably responsible for all the pierced noses of American punk rockers. This seemed quite likely to me. There had even been a band back in Chicago called Jagannatha Callas. As I remember, they were pretty good—shrill, but they rocked.

*

I don't want to give the impression that the trip was all good times. There were long hours in transit on trains so crowded you couldn't use the toilet because someone was sleeping in there. Trains so crowded you had to climb through the windows to exit at your stop. I remember a three-day bus trip—I don't remember where we were going, only the road-side shrines, where we paused to pay tribute in oil and flowers to those forces that could destroy the world by a simple dance or a random dream.

Hill stations, jungle towns, steamy river ports. Deserted resort hotels that seemed to have been painted upon the Indian shore by some ancient Vedic relative of Edward Hopper. Oceanside cities radiated wave after wave of heat back to the hot sky. Half-naked truck drivers at roadhouse tea stalls engaged in degraded versions of that same heated conversation. Cold beers were dispensed in weird bars. Fat whores and skinny beggars called to us at the entrance roads to towns and cities. There were villages where you had to be inoculated against unknown diseases before you could even enter. Everywhere people could be seen lined up at dawn, vomiting and pissing, brushing their teeth with chewed sticks and shitting in ditches. Monkeys chattered incessantly in night-time forests full of fireflies.

*

The vast distances, the dehydration, the sensory overload, the speed or lack of speed, the sleep or the lack of sleep—everything blurred together after a while. Mysore looked like Pestosore. Goripani looked like Juripanda. Forward motion seemed backward and movement was no different than memory and memory colored the future—everything that was new was really old, or much more than old. Things merged, then separated. The bus driver looked like the coconut vendor or the hotel desk clerk from another town. Even the hotel rooms began to blend in a hallucinatory blur. One blue room reminded you of another blue room, which, in turn, reminded you of a glass of blue kool-aid you drank as a kid, which reminded you of your mother's summer dress, which was also blue and somehow connected you in an Oedipal manner to that cool public pool water by which you first sat entranced at the sight of the edge of a bathing suit riding the upper inner thigh of the goose-pimpled wet flesh of some teenage girl you had a crush on.

Perverse or not, the narrative of associations should go on and on. The syntax of similarities, the discourse based on adjectives and shapes, surely had something to do with the irrationality of history, I thought—how the emotions of whole populations could be related to unperceived ancient suggestions, or the idea of *deja vue*, and the sense of past-life phenomenon, and other theories of "types" and "correspondences." Not that there was ever a guiding plan or purpose, but properties did resonate, and in the common pool of coded substances, crossroads could be found. The conscious human mind evolved in this manner. Let it all happen, I figured.

Sophie might have criticized such connectionist leanings on my part, but the technique was more common to her than me, and that heightened irrationality made her world-view more accurate than mine. She could see the relationship between a rhinoceros and a mandrake root, between a Ferris wheel and a fish eye, a polka and a mariachi. I wasn't so sure, but then, oddly, I *could* see it once she mentioned it. The universe has no law until we see law within it, then, eventually we see *only* what conforms to that law. In fact, our need for rule is what constitutes the rule. Change one little thing anywhere, and everything would be different. Everything is simultaneous in space and time. One does not really need to move.

Did we think we could actually learn anything about the world by *being* in it? Did we think this life we were passing through—India, Paris, Chicago—with its attendant blockbuster cast of thousands and all their dramas and beliefs had anything to teach? We sought to feed ourselves on the magnificent foreignness of everything, to bind ourselves together as if this visceral and sticky difference could actually act as glue. But the exoticism, the contradictions, in a word, the *reality* of India, served mostly as a springboard for further duels between us. That's how divorced we were. We may have argued over colonialism, Hinduism, reincarnation, but we had little idea what any of it meant. Connection with the culture was seldom made. India, like much of the rest of life, lay beyond us, out there somewhere, way out past our personal obsessions, our desires and drives.

*

Personally, I think the world is inscrutable. The only thing you learn is how you react to it—to beauty, death, disease. The confrontation with poverty on the subcontinental scale is really a confrontation with one's reaction to poverty—one's ability to feel guilt, or pity, or empathy, or, to shut it out entirely. That's what drives the tourist industry—the desire to feel anything at all. Sometimes it's better not to. Maybe the prophets of the television universe *are* right—it's enough to have it projected. You can read the travel books, the novels—try to regain the veil. But the point is to get away from that kind of second-order experience, to get back to a one-on-one relationship where everything is new and now. India did give us an illusion of newness—the strange combinations of taste, for instance: donuts coated with yogurt and black peppercorns; chilies in milk; lime pickle and salty curd. Convulsive beauty came to us in dishes served on stainless plates, in parades of orchids and horses, swans and lotus blossoms, floating candles and the dead bodies of martyred dreamers drifting like Ophelia down a milky Ganges stream of endlessly multiplying meanings.

There's an old saying you hear in the train stations and chai parlors: the world is soaked in consciousness like syrup. I came to believe that while sitting under the ceiling fans of some blue-tiled or rose-colored restaurant, the afternoon light subtly quivering about the room, the song of running faucets constantly playing, men gargling, plates clattering, the high, strident pitch of the local tongue, the distant if endless Bollywood soundtrack; it worked on my mind and I liked it. I liked watching Sophie lick the rose milk mustache from her lips. I didn't need to say anything about it. She liked my watching. Part of our bond was that we reacted to similar things in similar ways. We felt we had known each other before we met, and if we fought over differences, it was simply because we were able to, and if we suffered, it was temporal, something we knew to be an illusion. Time, after all, could be leaped over, in kicks and bounds, fighting all the way if need be.

*

One night in Madras I had a dream that seemed incongruous to everything that was going on: We were in Bernadette's apartment. She kept changing the channels on the TV, but all the shows were either about real domestic violence or fake exotic adventure. Bernadette didn't seem like herself—she had strange eyes and said things she wouldn't normally say, talking in some kind of L'il Abner corn-pone gibberish: "Golly bejesus Frankie boy. Ain't a goll durn good thing on Tellyvision to watch." Sophie was there, too. I remember someone called my name, "Frank!" I turned my head to see who it was, and that's when I noticed there were rows and rows of seats behind me, and a light beam from a projector. Then I realized I had been in a theater all along, sitting next to Sophie, but we were all much younger, teenagers maybe. We were watching *The Seven Voyages of Sinbad* with the Ray Harryhausen cyclops and the skeleton warriors. It must have been the 1960s. It was a big screen and everyone was happy.

Suddenly Sophie wasn't beside me anymore. It was some woman I didn't know who grabbed my hand and said, "Frank, this part scares me." Then, before I could reassure her, this thing came out of the shadows, some kind of sexually suggestive monster with the scaly body of a serpent, and an Opera Queen head topped with a magnificent headdress. Everything was moving in stop-action animation. All around the midriff of this Medusa a circle of hellhounds were barking constantly. I needed to ask the woman sitting next to me who the Medusa woman was, even though I didn't want to know. But every time I raised my voice, the dogs would react by climbing back into the Opera Queen's womb and they would kennel there cowering and crying. That sound collected itself and transformed into a song that became metallic if melodious:*"Ricordi il giorno tu la prima volta quando m'hai veduta? Signato abbiam celesti gioie in terra, insiem legati in sacro eterno amor!"* Which according to the dream translation meant: "the knot of the lover's heart begins as a noose that is turned by the Lady with Beautiful Hips."

*

I woke and stared at the white ceiling. Indeed, pieces of a puzzle seemed to be assembling, clues were to be found everywhere. And yet I didn't know if there was any point to it, if there was anything to look forward to that had not already happened. What I remember most, was a constant whispering back then, something I seemed to hear over my shoulder; it did not congeal, but rather sort of spun around in my head and heart like the white thread of an unknown storyline—perhaps because white is all frequencies, all possibilities, the color of insemination. Teresa of Avila was pierced, after all, by the white hot sword of Christ. Milton entered Blake's left foot as a white shooting star. The Minotaur was born of Persephone's infatuation with a white bull. A white elephant crept into the womb of Māyādevī of Sakya starting that whole epic process of self-annihilation. And I think there's a story about a great white rhinoceros that also started a religion in some country. Leda, of course, was loved by a swan, and St. Catherine was fed by a dove in prison. A stream of milk from Hera's breast created the stars. Hindus are obsessed with celestial dairy products. And, indeed, astronomy must have seemed like a dairy product contrasted with the darkness all around them. Lacrimosa Melancholia, I call it. Of course, it doesn't take a rocket scientist to figure out the symbolism—it all goes back to the caveman association of body fluids with protection, pools of water with mystical generation, ejaculations and emanations, and further back than that actually, back to breast fetishes, ancient mothers and the association of milk and semen and blood.

When I was a kid, I read about Haley's Comet in science books and often thought, "I will be such and such an age when that comet comes." It was a big deal in my child's mind to project myself into this future cosmic event as a witness, to stand in awe with my fellow humans as the ball of fire crossed the sky. Of course, I had no idea where, or even *if* I would live long enough to really see it, and I assumed it would be an act of will by which I would see it, and not a pure accident. But then one afternoon traveling up the coast from Bubaneshwar to Calcutta I looked out the train window imagining the landscape, its hills and crevices, as the giant body of a woman bathed in moonlight. And then, there it was—a white fireball on our right, rather pale, indistinct, hovering over the far away mountains and plains, moving faster than we could imagine, and yet it appeared absolutely still, as if to emphasize the relativity of time. I pointed to it and said "Haley's Comet!" I couldn't believe it. Neither could Sophie.

"You're crazy, Frank," she said. But she knew it was.

(six)

The Black Mother or Kali Ma, appears at first as the inky patch of anger on Durga's forehead. By most accounts her eyes are pink and her hair is ratty and dank. Her tongue is near nine feet long, and is said to loll and beat like a death knoll, signifying both arousal and shame. She eats rotten meat and slugs down blood red wine. Her breasts are pendulous and she is covered with skulls and severed limbs. Her earrings are corpses. Streams of blood flow ceaselessly about her thighs, which are rounder than banana trunks. They say to look at her is to have your soul rung like a rag—she demands that level of ardor.

The city of Calcutta begins in the legend of Sati's self-immolation.

Sati was Shiva's daughter. She was also his wife. She had been called Kali in another life, and she was also Uma. She would be reborn later as Parvati whose skin was black as sapphire. Following Sati's dismemberment, her left toe fell on the southside of Calcutta. Therefore, for the foot fetishist the city of Calcutta perhaps holds a certain erotic appeal, and if eroticism and leftism can be linked, perhaps Calcutta provides the map to do so: poetry and communism are practiced here, as is Tantra, the cult of erotic transcendence.

Calcutta was also, appropriately, the turning point in our journey of growing discontent. The incessant heat, the eleven-plus million people, the poverty, pushed us further in upon ourselves, making us devour each other in an embarrassing imitation of the hunger that surrounded us. Two people are two universes; when they collide they create a third universe, which is their life together. This life can be a star or a black hole, depending. We were the latter.

Our original plan was to visit the Sisters of Mercy Home for the Dying, where Mother Teresa ministered to the terminal. It was said you could volunteer to work there for a day or a year, and that it was a way for Westerners to relieve their guilt at being rich or pretty or simply being alive when most of the world was ugly, starving and dying. This was Mother Teresa's plan—comforting the losers while fostering Western attention. Sophie and I were going to do that one day—show mercy to the dying—but since it required getting up early in the morning, usually "tomorrow" was the day that our mercy would be shown.

The capital of Bengal has a reputation for being the most miserable city in the world. There are men in the Howrah train station with razor blades glued to their fingernails. We never went to the Howrah slums but we did go to the Kalighat temple. Apparently long ago human sacrifices were done there. Now they sacrifice a black goat instead; they cut its head off with Kali's sword. We didn't catch the actual act but we saw the abattoir, the *boli* enclosure. The goat has to be black. I'm not sure why. There were numerous people happy to offer their answers, their expertise and guidance. One of them, Sanjay Johnson, took us into the *boli*: it was marked out by a low wall surrounding two blocks of stone with an iron ring embedded to chain the animal's head. Old blood stained the stones and the stains swarmed with flies.

I wondered aloud if anybody eats the goat, or if they just throw it away. I suppose if they ate it, then that would negate its value as a sacrifice. Kali is supposed to get it, to appease her hunger. She drinks its blood and eats its "banana." Ma likes her bananas smeared with blood and sweets. The idea is that one thing stands in for another. In the creation of eternal time, a cucumber is worth an ox, and a banana dipped in blood is the same as a penis. The goat is lust, which stands-in for humanity in our earthly state. The whole of human thought is a great standing-in. The quest is to discover what for: God or emptiness, right or wrong, Chevy or Ford? That's where the goat comes in—as the goat head falls, so do the polarities of thought.

Sophie disagreed with the whole idea—not human sacrifice, but animal sacrifice—and she was quick to start an argument with Sanjay Johnson, who, to his credit, didn't see the point of arguing with this over-educated entitled American. Another guy standing in the shadows saw an opportunity and offered himself as a conversational/sacrificial victim before the wrathful sword of Sophie Walker/Wagner who was at this moment an avid campaigner for animal justice in a land where a rat could be your grandmother.

"What is it that you don't agree with?" the man asked. "There is no life without death."

"But what does this kind of killing do? There's no god that cares about this. It's barbarian."

"Maybe so, but whole civilizations are founded on it just the same. The Aztecs, the Greeks even, and you, too, as I assume you are a Christian." He said the word with a certain sneer.

The guy was about as tall as Sophie, rather thin, slightly dark-skinned and dressed in a loose fitting dhotee. He had a longish chin beard and was wearing some kind of turban contraption. But he didn't seem Indian to me.

"Yeah . . . and they are all dead. Dead civilizations, get it?" Sophie joked.

"They were around longer than your America, where the people are so high-minded they are shooting at Virgin Mary statues. Don't tell me there's no meaning in symbolic acts," the guy said while he made a chin-scratching gesture meant to symbolize inquisitive thought.

"How do you know about that Mary statue thing, anyway?" I asked.

"We have television here too, you know. You Americans think it's funny, with your guns and money, but you understand nothing."

"That shooter was a freak, it doesn't mean anything."

"Well, what about Jesus? Your own religion is based on sacrifice—pagan sacrifice, candy-coated as a gift from God."

"It's not my religion," she said.

"Oh sure," I said.

"Shut up." Sophie snarled, then turned back to our new antagonist. "I don't believe the crucifixion is what's really important, anyway—it's the birth. Mary is the transformer. It seems a small part, but it's really bigger. She's the one concerned with day-to-day human life. Jesus was nothing but a surrogate, a mask for a pompous sky daddy who doesn't really care for the people he created."

The guy rolled his eyes at me. "Whatever you say. Still, it's your western cult of decadence and acquisition," he said. "You mistake privilege for right. But you can't impose your liberalism on practices that date back thousands of years. You have no authority in that past or, for that matter, even in this present. Your ideas can only be born out of what came before, and your judgment is nothing but revised hindsight. Western morality is something you afford, not something you work toward or suffer for. India is far more tolerant than America in that respect."

She said, "Yeah, well, tolerance is a gift of privilege too. You can afford to tolerate others because you are not affected. If we were taking your jobs, it would be different. But we bring you money. So everyone accepts us." She flashed a roll of rupees. "That's not tolerance, it's economics."

Here again, I couldn't tell if she was agreeing or being contradictory. It did seem a bit conservative for her. Besides, I couldn't see the point of the argument. After all, it seemed to me people were getting slaughtered everyday just by living, in this city, and every other city.

So I put in my two bits.

"What about the ruined lives of workers in industrial societies? Can these be considered sacrificial? Are these spiritually dead men and women meant to appease some mechanical deity? Maybe God is a machine. I mean, it's just as easy to see it that way."

"The true pillars of religion are nameless," the guy said. He held out his hand. "My name is Sonny, by the way."

"Frank," I said, "This is Sophie."

"Pleased to meet you," he said.

Sophie was still pursuing the conversation. "Hey," she said, "The only real sacrifice is martyrdom—kill yourself. That's all it takes. That's all there is to it. Killing someone else is cowardice. I don't care what Levi-Strauss or Jean-Pierre Quelque Chose says. You can't justify murder with French structuralism."

Sonny looked at me with his slightly bloodshot eyes. This was well beyond what he had in mind to talk about when he first approached us—not that I knew exactly what that was.

Sophie went on: "Animals can't be made to take on human sins. If you want to create symbolic castration, well you . . . you ought to just castrate yourself, that's what you really mean anyway. See what I'm getting at?"

"Jesus Christ. Is this your wife?" Sonny interrupted, looking at me again with a kind of pleading look.

"Yes," I said to avoid complications. We always told people we were married. It was easier. Besides, we seemed married—our mutual antagonism gave us that married air. Of course, some people thought I was Sophie's father. She always got a laugh out of that.

"She acts like a wife," Sonny said, resignedly agreeing with my unspoken thought.

"Yeah?" said Sophie, smirking. "Who are you anyway?"

"I told you, my name is Sonny Valentine."

"Only an American would have a fake name like that."

And, indeed, it turned out he was American. The accent was adopted, the dark skin was a deep tan. He'd been in India for nearly ten years. He mostly lived in Benares but had come down to Calcutta to work with Mother Teresa, just like us—had not actually done so as yet, of course, but meant to, any day now. And to study tantra and communism. He was a radical of an admittedly lazy persuasion. He taught at some school or other.

"School of what?"

"Let's take a walk. I'll tell you what."

We took a walk. The shrine of Mother Kali was surrounded with devotees and we were unable to see anything but a brief glimpse of her golden eyebrows and scarlet tongue. Broken coconuts and red hibiscus flowers littered the ground around her feet. The coconut supposedly symbolizes the breaking of the self-will, Sonny said, as he urged us toward the exit of the compound.

Outside of the temple we wandered through the surrounding neighborhood. Everywhere artists were painting statues of Kali for the puja—little bloody cartoon statues and the larger botanica-sized statues. There were paintings and sculptures for sale. We passed through a fetid row of shops, past astrologers and palmists and barbers, to the ghat itself, the place of cremation at the water's edge. The Houghly proper had long since ceased to flow past this spot, and the water that remained was only a stagnant black canal. Sonny gave us some of the history as we gawked around, but he was more interested in asking questions, feeling us out.

"So you have come here for what?" he asked Sophie, "Adventure, holiday, or some kind of spiritual journey?"

"This is just something to do; it relieves the boredom," I said sarcastically. Sophie nodded as if in agreement, mostly to avoid answering.

Then she said, "What about you? What are you here for? Fleecing tourists?" She laughed.

But he was waiting for this question so as to launch into what seemed a well-practiced spiel. When he was in the States, he said, back in the early '70s, he got involved with some West Coast cult that considered the material world to be evil, something to be neutralized through indulgence, especially if the indulgence was sexual. But that was alright because Sonny believed that matter and consciousness were the same, or at least one does not negate the other. It meant the life of the flesh was still a valid spiritual path. Eventually he went off on his own because he realized neither discipline—dualism or onanism—provided exactly the rationalizations that he needed to pursue his secret agenda of procuring sexual favors from young women. I added this last part in my mind but I knew Sophie agreed.

Sonny went on. In India he got turned on to this 19th century mystic Ramakrishna, whose temple was here in Calcutta.

"Who?" Sophie asked.

"He is important to the tantric practice, and to Kali," he replied. "If you want, I can tell you some good books to read about him."

"We've got enough books," I said.

"Another California wacko," Sophie said, to the side.

Sonny ignored the comment. "The Great Swan has been dead for a hundred years," he said distractedly, shooing away some beggar children.

"Isn't he the guy on the posters in all the convenience stores?" I asked.

"That's Krishna Murti," Sophie corrected me with put-on authority.

"I don't know, they all look the same," I said. I made some head gestures and we both laughed.

Sonny was getting frustrated with our irreverence. But he convinced us to go to a bookstore with him. So we got in a rickshaw and went to the Oxford Bookstore on Park Street. He pointed out a whole shelf of books on various Hindu holy men—sadhus, gurus, lulus. We bought a book on this Ramakrishna guy because it cost almost nothing. Then we went back out in the street and walked around for a while, picking up our pace and hoping to tire this Sonny person out. He kept suggesting we buy something to eat, which actually meant buying him something to eat. We decided on tea alone, which we gulped when it had cooled enough.

"I'm getting hungry," he said, suggestively.

"Yeah, well we gotta get going," I said. I stood up and offered my hand. "Alright man, we'll see you later. Time for us newbies to get home. We burn up in this sun."

"Come and see me at the YMCA. I'm going to be in town for a month," Sonny said.

"Great, we'll see you again then," Sophie added. It was meant to blow him off, but it was also ironic because Sophie liked renegade mystics and dubious intellectuals, even if they were perverts; their confused take on the world matched hers. Maybe that's why she liked me.

"YMCA—it figures," she said, snickering as we walked away.

"We'd better get a rickshaw." The busses were overcrowded, and walking was time-consuming.

They were supposed to be building a subway in Calcutta, but no one seemed to be working on it. The tunnels flooded every monsoon and they spent the rest of the year waiting for them to dry out.

"He's a creep," I said.

"So are you."

"Me?"

"You don't want to visit him?"

I explained—it wasn't that I disliked the guy, but I didn't want reciprocal obligations eating up our time.

You make friends with someone like that and the next thing you know you're going to their house for dinner. Then you're babysitting their kids. Pretty soon you're bound and gagged in their basement and there's a ransom note delivered to the papers. No one pays attention though because you're not famous. All the good deeds you were going to do never get done. Years pass. Eventually they find your bodies when the building gets torn down to build a new shopping mall or apartment complex. That wasn't going to happen to us. We had plans. We wanted to take the Rajdani Express to Delhi and backtrack to Agra and up to Varanasi from there. Our visas were good for three months. We didn't have time to be tied up or die.

We were headed back to the hotel when I thought I heard someone yelling Sophie's name. I turned and saw this Sonny character also in a rickshaw pursuing us down the street, kicking up a cloud of dust. Sonny was standing in the seat like some kind of subcontinental Ben-Hur looking over the heads of the crowd, weaving through the traffic of Mirza Ghalib. Some dogs were chasing his rickshaw and a couple kids were running after the dogs, and it seemed like some goats were chasing the kids, and the goat's owners were chasing the goats, and their kids were chasing them. It just went on and on as if he were pulling a train of the world's misery along with him.

"Miss Sophia, Miss Sophia," he cried, waving something in the air. I told our wallah to slow down, as if he could really go any slower. Sonny pulled along side of us. He was waving a book around. It was the Ra-makrishna book. She had left it in the tea shop.

"Thanks," she said. He handed it to her, clasping her hand at the same time in that sicko hand-clasp all women know.

"You must come and visit me, come sometime this week, we will talk. I don't get to speak with Americans much." That seemed like a lie. He probably spoke to Americans every day. But we let it go. He turned off and went down a different street while we got caught in a traffic jam of bicycles waiting for an elephant to cross the road.

Back at our hotel I said, "I think Sonny's got a crush on you."

"Probably. All men are sleazy."

"Yeah, but if they didn't pay any attention to you, you'd be pissed." It was the wrong thing to say and I knew it, which might be why I said it—I'm pretty sure I didn't really believe it. Sophie could let a lot of things go by—it was part of the great general joke of the universe—but there were times when she would pick up on the smallest inconsequent or perceived slight and become absolutely enraged.

"See, that's exactly the fucking problem."

"What?"

"That you think so. That women like it. And that gives men license to do it." She looked disgusted. Then she stuck out her tongue. Suddenly she was extremely unhappy. "I don't even know what I'm doing here."

"Life's an adventure," I said, mocking Sri Valentine,

"a search for spiritual teaching."

"For you, maybe," she laughed.

"C'mon, you wanted to come, too."

"You wanted to. I came with you. Don't blame me."

"But you *were* interested at least, weren't you?"

"That's what you want to believe. Apparently I don't have anything to do with it. I wanted to go to Italy."

"Italy? Really? Funny how you never mentioned that."

"See, you don't even know. You assume you know what I want. You should have known."

"Jesus," I said.

She was joking, sort of, but it was also partially true, or at least it was becoming true. We seemed to be bound more by anxieties than by shared attitudes toward life. We were two different wavelengths bouncing around a room together. Like Didi and Gogo from *Godot*, we often joked about the day we would break up. But we needed each other despite the difficulties, or maybe because of them. So in a way it was easier to say, "Let's go our separate ways," knowing we wouldn't actually act on it. We could always break up tomorrow.

"I think we should break up when this is over," she said.

"Yeah, you're right. But what do you want to do now."

"I guess get something to eat."

And it always went like that—half joke, half warning—but then this was precisely the place where it probably *would* happen. The pressure of the inconve-

nience might force the event, the way lighting a cigarette at a restaurant will make the food come. And of
course the stakes were highest because of the difficulty.
Sophie could prove she didn't need me, more than ever,
right now. She could do it anytime, but now would be
ideal in the most inconvenient way for both of us.

"Whatever you want to do," I said. "Just actually do
something, one thing or the other."

"That's just it, I've never done anything of my own
volition. I've always followed along with other people's
plans."

"You're getting too serious. Let's eat," I said. "I'm
suddenly hungry."

"You sound like that Sonny dude now."

Of course, I did sound like Sonny. And she did want
to eat, too. So we did. While we sat waiting for our goat
biryani, I wondered if it would be one of the goats sac-
rificed at the temple. Maybe all these restaurants got
their meat from sacrificial animals. While I was having these thoughts I realized I wasn't listening to Sophie—although I am sure she was talking. Instead, I
was thinking how maybe our coming to India might
have been a good thing. But then I thought that was a
selfish thing to think. And then I thought the thought
that "thinking it was selfish" was itself, selfish. Obviously I had to drop this circular train of selfish thought
or I would go mad from the redundancy.

It's a corny truth that love may be the last adventure for humans on this dying earth. Skid row is crowded with failed romantics and tantric heroes, impotent

saints and derailed Indiana-Jones type lovers—people who didn't break on through to the other side Jim Morrison style, or any other style. Or they broke through and there was nothing there. You can't rescue anyone either. You can, however, take on their flaws as a form of relief. You can lift their burden by becoming their burden, and then you can excuse yourself. It all seems so noble and it happens so fast—the slide I mean. Maybe things aren't going well. You get a messianic complex. You go to the movies, you go to the park, you go to some nice tourist town where everybody's happy. You think to yourself, well we've gone this far, let's keep going. The world's a big place, everything is so big; our problems should look small in comparison. But it's not true. Nothing matters but individual obsessions, like worms feeding on the lies behind your face, making it do strange things in the mirror.

(seven)

According to Vedic cosmology, the earth is ringed by concentric oceans. First is the ocean of salt, followed by sugar-cane juice, then wine, clarified butter, milk, whey, and finally fresh water. The gods churn the ocean with a giant serpent. Things begin to appear: the moon, the goddess Sri, the white horse of the sun, a magnificent gem, a great elephant, then the deadly poison, which Shiva drinks to save the world. The poison gets trapped in his neck. Durga drinks this poison to become Kali.

Some days our lives were like a bad existential play—No Exit from Bubaneshwar or Waiting for Marty Singh.

"What are we gonna do today, Sophie?" I might say.

"I don't know. What do you wanna do today, Frankie?"

"I don't know. Does it matter?"

"Does anything matter?"

"Well at least we're sure of one thing, then—nothing matters. So there is certainty after all."

Indeed, I may have been as lonely in her company as she might have been in mine. I believed, however, that her loneliness/indecision was primarily based on her perception that I was engaged in a theft of her will. Even when I offered that will to her on a platter:

"I'll do what *you* want to do."

"What do I want to do?"

"I don't know. You choose." I said it over and over again.

"No, you."

"You're always saying I choose everything we're going to do, so I'm letting you," I said, trying to stop the next response.

"*Letting* me? Thanks."

"That's not what I meant, and you know it."

"What did you mean then?"

"I didn't mean anything by it."

"Maybe you should start, meaning something." That sounded like an insult, I showed the proper concern with an anguished facial expression. "Forget it," she said.

"Look, what do you want?"

"I don't know. You tell me what I want. That seems to be what you want."

Whole days would pass this way—we might wake up in a different town, a different country even—the conversation would be the same, as if there had been no break in our mundane need to fill the void.

We spent a lot of time reading. I read my Hindu Classic Mythology Comics starring Shiva and Vishnu. Sophie read the book on the life of Ramakrishna. I think the title was *Life of the Paramahamsa*, or something like that. Apparently his descent into the mystic profession was actually rather will-less.

"This guy sounds like me," she once said, "only he's really fucked up."

"Really? Did he have trouble making decisions

too?" I forced a laugh.

She mirrored it. "Ha ha. Look who's talking."

"We have to do something pretty soon," I said, "the hotel guys are getting suspicious. We have to leave the room, eventually."

"Why?"

"I don't know. Visions are waiting to be had. Cash is waiting to be thrown away. The world waits. Name your quest."

"Arguing is such a fulfilling passion, who needs vision?"

"We do!" I answered in a somewhat desperate tone. "We need to see beyond ourselves."

"I'm done with this," she said. "What are we talking about?"

"C'mon, let's keep it going."

"Look. I just don't want to visit that guy Sonny, if that's what you're getting at. There's something weird about him. I don't know what it is. He seems a little too, I don't know, interested."

"Hey, I never wanted to anyway. I figured you did."

"I never said that."

"Alright. So, we won't. I don't care," I said. But somehow I knew it was inevitable that we would. There have been studies that show a driver on the highway will unwittingly steer toward the stalled car on the road shoulder, and this hypnotic attraction is the cause of many seemingly unexplainable accidents.

I heard dogs barking outside, as the sound was carried down the various hotel halls and passages that led to our door. "I know what you mean though. He is a little off, a little lascivious. Is that the word?"

She gave me the eye.

We were staying in a blue room in a place called the Maria Hotel, which was down a passage in a courtyard not far off Sudder Street in Chowringhee, close to the New Market. One day we went into that market to have our photos taken so we could get trekking permits. We also needed to get Nepalese visas. It was a whole day of activities and it filled us with a sense of purpose. The YMCA wasn't hard to find after that. It was like a magnet and we pretty much walked right up to it without even trying. I could smell the laundry and hear the rattle of the cups and plates in the kitchen a block away. Sonny was standing out front with some guys in white shirts all of whom left when they saw us. "Hey Baba," he exclaimed, "glad you came by!"

"We didn't mean to come by, it was an accident."

"No accident. Fate," he said. "Kismet. Let's go inside and have some tea."

If it was fate, we slid into it. Fate was our grace at this moment. He took us into a large white room under a ceiling fan. Somebody brought the tea without anyone asking.

"Sonny Valentine—that's not your real name is it?" I said, as an icebreaker. I wanted to start the conversation out tough, insightful, but tender.

"Does anybody have a real name?"

"Does anybody really know what time it is?" Sophie asked mockingly.

"Look, we don't have any money, if that's what you're after."

He ignored my comment. "I mean a true name is something you create, isn't it?" he said. "One should choose a name that embodies who you see yourself becoming, then you grow into it. All free will starts with naming." Obviously, he didn't want to tell us his real name, but he was willing to explain the fake one.

He had been in love apparently, in the days of his reckless youth, etc., etc. She ended it in a bad way. He nearly let it kill him, spending years in alcohol abuse and cult therapy groups, raking through the ashes of his past while searching for the source of his future failures. He found it a thousand times over, too, and lost it just as many. He was randy in his decisions and over-invested in his intuitions. One day he wanted out of the circle of pain. Like a lot of 70s types, he tried his hand at different religions—the Process, the Mooneys, the Krishnas, the New Carpathians, and the Mani-Marians, which he claimed was a branch of the Latter Day Epicurians.

"The New What? The Latter Day Who?" Sophie asked.

"I told you about them before, remember, some gnostic, new-age freaks." (He hadn't told us, but it didn't matter.) "But they were into some sick shit." I saw Sophie's ears tilt. At the same time something registered on Sonny's face. The first subtle thread of a bond was forming, a web of psychological attachment, and he was going to pull gradually upon it. This wasn't a good thing.

"Yeah? Like sick what?" she asked.

I could see the wheels turning in his head, game plans adapting, as new sentences were forming. For all I knew his entire story changed right at that moment. He could have been launching into the biggest lie he'd ever concocted. I know I would have, with suckers like us to play—who wouldn't?

Sonny went on. "It was Oregon, in the '70s. Their gig was based on the idea of destroying one's attachment to the senses and the emotions they generated. You could do this by indulging those senses to the extent they ceased to have any meaning. Think of it like saying a word so often that it becomes nonsense and finally it's just empty sound. That emptiness is truth. In the same vein, you exhaust emotion, exhaust pleasure. Eventually you arrive at the empty mirror, and that is also truth."

"So truth lies in exhaustion?" I said, "Then we must be wise indeed, cause I'm tired as hell." I feigned sleepiness, thinking maybe it was a way to go home.

"Ha ha." Sophie kicked me under the table. "So, where does your exhaustion philosophy come from?" She was intrigued.

"Valentinus. I took him as my model for many years. But the problem was the anti-moral, anti-social ethic— to my mind it suggested all kinds of criminal possibilities. Orgies were one thing, but eating fetuses was something else."

"You're kidding, right?"

"Of course . . . I'm kidding." He said this while gazing intently down at some fascinating dust mote in the window light.

"That's disgusting," I said. "How did they taste?"

We didn't believe any of this, but went with it anyway. Then Sophie added, "I can see it now—aborted fetuses pureed in a blender with ginseng and tofu." We all laughed alone at our different sick fantasies.

Then Sonny stopped laughing and went back to talking. "So then I was in Portland for awhile, Portland, Oregon. It's a good town because nobody's paying attention to you—anything goes. Got involved with these transvestites—they had this house on, I think, Northwest Harrison. Real party animals, but at least they *were* religious about it. But what with all the strangers, the syphilis, the herpes, the dope, and the money, it got so I didn't know what was going on around the building, who was being paid and who was paying, who was dying and who was lying.

"Then one day I met this woman, Annabelle Lee, at least that's what she called herself. She took her name from a Poe poem. She was dark in that mental way, if you know what I mean, dark and ready, and she needed to take me somewhere I didn't want to be. I don't know if it was Satanic on her part or merely deeply pessimistic. I got into it a little bit, but then I started trying to back out. But she wouldn't let go easily. Then one night when I came home—I hadn't seen her in a month or more—and there she was, hanging out in the stairwell of my hotel on Burnside. She was all dirty, and her hair was all matted like she'd been sleeping outside and her teeth were all yellow. She said, 'Sonny, you haven't finished with me yet.'"

It sounded like a normal night in the Burnside district to me. But Sonny claimed it changed his life. He threw himself at decadence and self-hatred. He became a whore-monger, a debauchee, much like the Young Augustine, with Burnside as his Carthage. Sonny would use the Augustine allusion again and again. In fact, you might say that, among the many reasons to doubt his character, one was this rather easy identification with high-level religious figures. But we were shoppers, we were in it for the story, and so we held back our criticism.

"I realized," he went on, "that a man could not be free unless he conquered his fears—whether of women, men, bestiality, God or emotional sadism. Mine was a fear of my own depravity, my own shame. I decided to indulge it."

So Sonny Valentine was reborn as a holy man, as if he had stepped right out of the pages of some Carson McCullers novel, preaching his ideas to the bums of skid row, freeing the poor up to enjoy each other in love and pleasure. That's how he described it. Then one night he had a dream of St. Christopher as a dog-headed hobo, standing in the middle of the Burnside bridge, reciting "The Hymn of the Pearl" to a gathering of other dog-headed, one-eyed men with their huge mouths and endless hungers. They were all travelers, the saint said, bearing the burden of Cain through the material world. And it was this dog-headed preaching dream hobo who told Sonny that what he was looking for was right in front of him, and that all he needed to do was recognize it.

Sonny asked if we knew the Hymn. We didn't. So he recited a bit: "As I gazed on it, suddenly the garment seemed to be a mirror of myself, I saw in it my whole self, and in it I saw myself apart, there were two entities, but one form." He went on to say that the important message here was the duality within the unity, which he would later connect, both to St. Bernard's "garment," and the non-dual Shaivism he would discover in Benares.

The day after the dream, he said, he was visited by a middle-class redhead who was in town for some "Tantra and You" convention. She'd heard something about Sonny and decided to look him up. Where she would have heard about him is a mystery, as he was really a local phenomenon. She introduced herself as Tara Ravi, *tantrica*. She was looking for like-minded people to form a school of ecstatic redemption—for a fee, of course. The goal was essentially this: to remove the veil of illusion, and to understand that the body was the abode of bliss—something along that line. A lot of people had already signed up. Physical pleasure is an easy hook; that's why capitalism works so well.

This philosophy mostly seemed like a rationalization for an orgy, I thought, and I said so. Sonny chuckled. It did sound more sophisticated in memory, he admitted. Sophie frowned. Sonny went on.

He said this Tara-Ravi woman was a knockout—

she had bread, friends in high places and easy morals, making the package easy to swallow. And, of course, the decadence itself was hard to refuse. Poor Sonny got hooked and he suffered for it. One day he caught his Tara in a *ménage a quatre* with some nubile young disciples. Liberalism took a tumble and Sonny took a walk. He even considered changing his name to Werther as a reminder of the foolishness of devoting one's life to the unattainable—Sonny Werther, Man of Sorrows.

His original name, in answer to our old question, had been Mark.

"Mark Valentine?"

"No, man, Mark Smith, from Omaha." He chose Valentine in honor of the philosopher who had seen the Logos appear in a vision as a red baby seated on a throne and crowned with gold and rubies.

Sophie didn't believe him, but she liked the over-reaching, the absurd plot development.

"Have you read anything in the Ramakrishna yet?"

"Only a little. It seems mostly like he passed out a lot."

"So what were you preaching to the bums?" I asked. "The School of Passing Out?"

"What else? Sell the people what they already want—the salvation of intoxication, the cruelty and deception of appearances. No one should believe that the world is safe or permanent. To embrace Kali is to rid yourself of all illusion. The true hero is the one who can have intercourse with their worst fear, with death and physical decay, which, down on Burnside, quite naturally translates into fucking the ugliest, most frightening person you can find just to prove to yourself that you can do it—that you can conquer the illusions of the flesh and of beauty."

"That's bullshit," Sophie interjected.

"Is it?" Sonny raised a cartoon eyebrow while modulating his voice. "Is it really?"

"Seems to me, most people are forced in that direction anyway," I threw in. "You're married too long. You're lonely in a strange city were everyone is ugly. I been in those towns. You're drunk. There's a whole number of ways it can go. You do it out of desperation, not inspiration."

"Perhaps. There is an element of interpretation, as you say. But, there's also the matter of choice, controlling how it happens. After all, it's only will-power that separates the hero from the householder."

"All this sounds like testosterone posing as religion," Sophie said. She was right in a way. But then, in typical Sophie Walker fashion, she turned right around and agreed with him. She said the same was true of women; they'd go out with a man who disgusted them. One reason was self-hatred—to punish themselves.

"A very Catholic interpretation," I said, although I did understand that you also did it to defeat it, to defeat the fear, which might be more Nietzsche than Christ.

"Of course, another reason is money," Sophie put in.

"Or power," I added.

"Whatever. It's the same thing. Most guys will fuck anything that's available: a whore, the school slut, sheep, a cat, a hydrocephalic." She laughed at her joke, as it happened that a hydrocephalic was walking past the window right then.

"Very inconsiderate," I said. "How un-PC."

"Get over yourself," she said.

We continued to argue in front of this Sonny fellow as if he weren't there. It's a good way of getting people to leave when you want them to leave—start a domestic disturbance. Sonny just smiled until we ran out of steam; then it was all about him again, our drama being a mere parenthetical bleep to his ongoing presentation.

He went on: faced with that humiliation of betrayal, he decided to shed his western ethics completely. He traveled for a while in India. He claimed he wanted to contrast tantra, as he knew it, with various aspects of Valentinian Gnosticism, and to draw a relationship between the female deities, specifically Kali and the lower Sophia, or the "Wisdom-Whore" as he called her. It was here in Calcutta he learned of "The Great Swan," Ramakrishna. He read some books about the saint and decided to settle down and study. The life of Ramakrishna seemed to present an interesting path: erotic stimulation with no actual sex or emotional involvement, just identification with deity. It put one smack in the center of the carnal world, then backed off with a certain Christian monkishness bordering on masochism. "You channel the energy to the head," he said, "where its release becomes a kind of symbolic castration."

"But you live in Benares now, right?" I asked.

That was true. He had recently become interested

in the Kashmiri school of non-dual Shaivism, which is based on the dynamics of the three-part heart of Shiva.

We didn't ask for it but here it was:

This school believed that ignorance was the attachment to polarities. But all polarities create a rhythm, a ticking pendulum, if you will, of expansion and contraction, which is analogous to the throbbing of consciousness. The pulse is so rapid, however, that its poles are virtually simultaneous, thus verging on stillness, a still seam where all oppositions are mended, a state of ecstasy along which, "Shiva strings himself like a vine."

This was way too esoteric for me and I said so: "I don't get it."

"It's a sound, the sound of the Goddess within Shiva's heart. So you see it all ties together," he said.

It did seem to, especially if you weren't paying close attention. Lack of attention makes the world seem whole.

So now the ultimate Sonny Valentine legacy was to create a synthesis. In Benares, he was continuing work on what he called "The Valentinian Speculations," which he was sure he would publish one day, although at the moment these mostly amounted to several cardboard boxes filled with both typed and hand-written manuscripts, accumulated for some twenty years and dating from long before he left the States.

The sky was darkening outside the Salvation Army. Sonny had taken on that aura of the pervert-scholar, the cult-leader, the sociopath among the sheep. And Sophie had, by this point, taken a genuine interest, which to Sonny meant she was hungry, which would eventually lead to a kind of desperation. To facilitate that desperation he would leave her hungry; or maybe he just couldn't carry on the charade any further. The result was the same. The problem with Westerners like ourselves, Sonny said, was that, "You are pulled in too many directions trying to find what works for you, patching together a spirituality without a path, without learning how to get there. You think you can shop for it. In America, that's what you're told from the day you're born. I know. I tried."

"It sounds like you are still trying," I said.

"Well, you got me there." He got up. He had to be someplace. I saw a guy waiting for him at the door. The guy looked anxious just like Sonny did. Sonny had been anxious the whole time. It was an anxious place, full of spiritual anxiety.

*

Sophie and I decided to walk back. It didn't seem far, and it would give us time to talk. On a broad commercial avenue—I don't remember the name—we saw a crowd gathered. It was barely noticeable, considering. They were watching some street performer. From a distance a woman appeared to have a little monkey tied on a string, who danced while she played music on a high, shrill, double-reed shenai whose sound carried far beyond its immediate environs.

"Let's go look at the monkey," I said. But it wasn't

a monkey; it was a human kid. Probably female, but it was hard to tell. The child had no arms and it was holding a tin cup in its teeth for coins. It came up to Sophie and danced around in a desperate way that was worse than a horror movie. The evil pervading the scene was actually our innocence framing it. Maybe innocence and evil are both illusions. Maybe our disgust was an illusion too. I wanted to think I was a moral person.

"Too bad," I said, "but nothing we can do about it." I thought I was being realistic.

"You're an asshole," she said."

"Everyone is. That's the truth." But I was lying. I didn't believe in truth and neither did she. We'd seen legless men walking on blocks of wood and armless men using toes and sticks to eat. We'd joked about it. But this scene disgusted us more because of the maternal complicity.

Sophie called me out for cowardice. "You just don't want to think about your own place in relation to the world's pain."

I was trapped. So I called her out for romanticizing human nature. "Desperation can drive anyone to extremes," I said. "People have to eat. Why should a human be treated any different than an animal? After all, cavemen ate their children's brains. Many animals starve their young. Friends destroy their friends to survive. Do you think our friends care anything about us? It's all about the result, not the path. Everything is forgiven if it provides entertainment," I said. "Celebrities prove this is true every day."

"And this is entertainment?" she asked in a Jewish mother imitation that deflated the scene.

Well, if it wasn't, *we* certainly were. Once again people were watching us argue.

"Look," I said, "There's the audience, even for us." I was sweeping my arm across the spectacle in a grandiose operatic gesture. She didn't seem to think it was funny. She said no mother should treat a child this way, and that I had no empathy. I said motherhood wasn't holy, and how could she know anyway, never wanting to be a mother.

This was a bad road to go down, but there we were, way down it. "Fuck you," she said.

I said, "You hate your own mother because you were born, and now you don't want to be hated so you don't want to be a mother. It's not concern for overpopulation, it's just selfishness."

She turned it around claiming I was angry at the very real possibility of never being a father, which is odd because I never thought I wanted to be a father, that is until she said she didn't want to be a mother, then fatherhood was suddenly *the* great emptiness in my life.

"If you want to have kids you'll have to find someone else," she said.

"You're trying to make this about us."

"It's not?"

"It's supposed to be about them."

"That's your tactic," she said, "to switch it like that—you can't stick to one approach. You get lost in your own rationalizations."

Truth is I *was* lost. The sight seemed to demand a moral interpretation and I was unable to produce one in the presence of this other person to whom my moral opinion might matter. I didn't know how to react. If I feigned indifference, then I had to justify the indifference. On the other hand, outrage without action would ring hollow. But I had to make a show of at least having considered the situation of being affected by it. My power, if I had any, lay in the fact that I wasn't alone. Of course, she was in a similar place. At a loss for moral ground, we decided to treat the event as a mere image to be critiqued, like an art object. So it was entertainment after all. Art for art's sake, life for art's sake. This was more than romantic, it was our prerogative, as well as a pretense—even if it did make us appear as phonies. All our rhetoric, we conceded, was a disguise for our fundamental lack of conviction. But there was a catch; if we could fake all this, we could fake anything—even affection. Hell, why not fake the whole relationship? After all, maybe we were only in it to kill time. This dancing child, like dancing Kali, was killing cosmic time. Sophie and Frank were killing mundane time.

We were so self-involved that when we came to, or rather out of our argument, we were standing in the same place. Time had passed and we hadn't noticed. We thought we had walked away, but we hadn't. The people around us were a bit bewildered by the irrelevant loudness of our conversation. Who did we white Westerners think we were anyway? Our self-involvement had taken attention away from the beggars, and that only brought into higher relief the superficiality of our concerns. What is identity compared to hunger? The little armless nameless girl was still dancing in front of Sophie, but it wasn't for money. It was almost as if she was trying to stop us, to ask us to please stop arguing, for the sake of the universe itself. If it wasn't for people like us, abstracting everything, maybe then there would be food enough for everyone.

We ignored her plea. "I can't take this." Sophie said. "Not everything is about you."

"I never thought it was. I always thought it was about you," I said.

We walked away. But we didn't stop. Sophie was walking several feet ahead of me using my body as a back-facing shield from the multiplying entourage of ragged children who were now following us.

When we got back, we didn't eat dinner. We read and we brooded. Maybe it was the stress. The next day we bought tickets to Benares, thinking that would help. Oddly enough, I thought I saw Sonny Valentine at one of the stations on down the Varanasi line. But I could have been wrong. In any case, whoever it was, he disappeared into the crowd. If it *was* Sonny, maybe he didn't want to talk with us anymore, either.

(eight)

Holi, at the end of Winter, is also, coincidentally, the celebration of the burning of Kama, who now revived, moves through the world as spirit and infection. He was said to live in the moon and in the mangoes. He could take the form of an erotic tree or be heard as the sound of bees. It was by the buzzing of Kama's bees that Shiva was inspired to make love passionately to the most beautiful of all women, the stunning Parvati. They made love for more than a thousand years without end. It was a love that frightened the gods.

Approaching Benares by morning train, my first vision was a pack of dogs ripping apart some carcass on the hazy plains outside the city. One of the dogs, trotting across the scrub was holding what seemed to be the animal's heart in its mouth, and in my half-sleep that heart seemed to be beating. My second vision was a band of red boys spitting red saliva on the sidewalk around the hotel. At first I thought it might be a tuberculosis epidemic, and that it had been a mistake to come here. But they were having too much fun to be consumptive.

We took a room in a hotel on the outskirts of the Brahma Nala district. There was a restaurant on the ground floor that from all appearances was never used, except as a hangout for local teenagers. Outside our room there seemed to abide a troupe of demonic flesh-eating monkeys, cackling like the hideously in-bred race from some H.P. Lovecraft novel. They kept trying to get inside, scratching at the shutters, prying at the window jambs with sticks. When they were not around, we went to the roof and watched the cacophonous vultures swirling over the chaotic city. You could hear the people beating their pots and pans, adding to the drone that rises from the urban cauldron of Kashi.

Varanasi, or Kashi as it used to be called, is a city famous for paan, a supposedly mild narcotic, which I, of course, absolutely had to obtain. The woman selling the paan looked vaguely like an old girlfriend, but that wasn't the reason for my patronage. I thought I would get high. But Sophie said I looked like a clown or a cannibal, that my red mouth was disgusting and that it made her anxious. I said she was exhibiting a culturally conditioned response and that she ought to open up, free her mind. I offered her some. She declined. Later as we walked the streets, I was attacked by a sacred cow—in plain sight—it went right for me. I dodged the horn but Sophie blamed it on my red clown mouth, claiming that I looked like a flesh-eater and the cow was taking aim.

We visited the Durga Temple. We watched the bathers at dawn in the Ganges, and the worshippers who floated oil wick lamps out onto the dirty waters. We watched the bodies burn on the ghats. One day we were arguing on a street corner. It had started with Sophie contrasting Kali to Saturn, or rather the conflict between humankind devouring time, and time devouring humankind. I said it didn't matter, time is a construct of the fallen psyche—it exists only because we think about it. She called that a Christian idea and said that time was actually a product of complexity and bifurcation. I said I had no problem with that.

The whole thing had started out, simply enough, as an argument with a cab driver who tried to overcharge us. The meter was running and we weren't moving. I didn't know what we were being charged for—space or time. This turned into a disagreement about how such things didn't matter in the long view. I won't pretend to trace the intersections, but the argument graded subtly into a disputation over Bernadette and her laissez-faire attitude toward self-promotion. Apparently, I should have taken Sophie's side in some argument that I didn't even remember, but, which Sophie assured me, was integral to the power structure of our relationship. This brought up further forgotten hostilities causing Sophie to raise her voice, which attracted the attention of strangers. That's when a Varanasi cop asked us up to keep it down. He thought we were going to get violent.

The cop, Rajinder Singh, was curious about our aggressive relationship, and he invited us to buy him dinner. In exchange he would warn us about scams going down in the city, con artists who prayed on tourists, etc. He did too—he told us murder stories involving drug deals and drug runners and daughters lost to drugs and one-legged counterfeiters of drug money and geo-political drug conspiracies. He seemed particularly focused on the drug scene. He was either trying to stir up a sense of danger or he was trying to sell us something. He threw off several names of hotels and it was difficult to tell if it was a warning or a sales pitch.

As we grew less comfortable, he grew more so, and the more comfortable he felt the more interest he showed in Sophie. He kept saying she could make a good living as a model. In Benares? Modeling? Yep, he said, legitimate business, on the up and up and all that. He happened to know someone, and they were always looking for western women to sell certain products, or to act on TV shows, or be walk-on comedians, as apparently the presence of a Westerner was a gag unto itself, turning a dire scene into comic relief. This pitch didn't make much sense to me, but then neither did it make sense when Rajinder dropped by our hotel the next day, especially since we hadn't told him where we lived. He asked if we wanted to visit his special holy place in the city, a real Varanasi experience he said. He would show us some other sights, too, as part of the bargain, absolutely free.

"Maybe tomorrow or Friday," I said.

"Okay," he said. "Here's the address." And he gave some number on such and such a boulevard in the Forest of Bliss.

Thursday we visited the Manikarnika Kund, the ancient bathing tank where Sati's earring supposedly fell to earth as she flew across the heavens like a cosmic kidnap victim. The water seemed filthy as it always does in these bathing tanks, but we ate lunch there and argued about the propriety of washing your underwear in a sacred pool.

Friday we went to visit Rajinder. We made our way through what had once been main streets but now seemed like back alleys. We were in the central part of the old city surrounded by a new town. Somewhere behind the Tripurabhairavi ghat we came to a large carved wooden door with a number painted on it. There were small stone Ganeshas, one on either side, both covered with red powder. A woman squatting by the door made various gestures that I interpreted as an inquiry into our business. "Rajinder," I said. The name sufficed. She sent a boy from the street running up the wet stone steps in clip-clops. He came back a minute later. We went in. The cop was there. So was another guy.

"I was hoping you would come." Rajinder got up. He was animated, anxious. "I am anxious to make you comfortable," he said, completing my thought. "Sit, sit." There were pillows all over the floor, and if you didn't sit you would probably trip. "Call me Raj," he said.

The other guy, Jada Chatterjee, as he was introduced, was a slovenly looking man, probably in his early fifties, but he could have passed for younger. He was propped up on pillows and never moved. He had an unusually wide mouth, pudgy fingers and a grapefruit-shaped bald head. He was dressed in perfumed silks and attended to by a young boy who brought him tea and rubbed his feet with oil. Jada gave me the willies. Every once in a while he addressed us in a slow, phlegmatic English.

"You are enjoying of Indian country, I think," he

said, "You will know many good things. Here wisdom comes for you and much adventures new and ancient." He lowered his head.

"Well, we need it," I responded.

"What are things you see that must interest you here? You are in our City of Light. For you, very excellent. Very good." He lowered his head again.

Sophie said she wanted to learn more about Tantra. She believed this was a specialty of Benares.

"Ah, the Tantra," he nodded knowingly, but said no more. In fact, it appeared he had fallen asleep. His boy took the teacup out of his slumping hand.

Raj kept the conversation going, switching from tourist niceties, to drugs and finally to sex, or rather sex cults and the young sex enthusiasts who came to Varanasi to get it on with the gods of love. He said we must be careful of the many false sex gurus who would take our money and our virtue.

"Those are many," he said, "who start high-minded and end with a taste for what we call the three P's: pedophilia, prostitution, and profit." His eyes lit up on the last two syllables.

The Grapefruit-Head, momentarily awake, laughed a little, "It is easy to lose one's way," he mumbled. Then he lowered his head again.

I noticed another guy, some long-hair, sitting against the wall with his eyes wide open—eyes that looked like blank dinner plates. He had previously blended in completely with the wall and he never blinked or moved. I gestured toward the guy. Raj said the world had no meaning for this man. "But you are not as the many," he said looking at Sophie. "I can tell. I think this is true. You are smart and not foolish. You seek meaning."

"Really? How?" she asked. "How do you know?"

"What? Do I look like the professor?" Rajinder laughed.

The Grapefruit-Head nodded knowingly. Then a woman came to the door and said something in Hindi or Bengali. Raj nodded. Then the funniest thing happened: our old pal Sonny Valentine walked in. "My friends!" he said with great enthusiasm.

Then he looked at me. "Baba!" he said, "Mr. Frank," and he made as if to bow. Turned out they knew each other, Rajinder Singh and Sonny Valentine—old pals. Sophie was surprised. For some reason, I was not. Sonny was wearing loose fitting pajamas and a vest. Another guy came in almost immediately after him and he was dressed in purple with a head wrap. We were never told his name. Someone else had some bitter liquor in a bottle. Another guy had a bag of fried chili peas. It was a party. Then the hashish came out. We declined the latter. Things were happening fast.

"Many people come for the hashish and the bhang."

"Yeah, well we don't do drugs," Sophie said, like they were going to believe that.

"I see, then maybe you want the 'hair-o-ween'?"

"No thanks, I had mine this morning," I said. It was a bad joke. The two men looked at each other quizzically.

Sophie laughed. "That's a dumb joke, Frank."

"Miss Sophia, my friend, you look a little thin. You have been sick, perhaps?"

"Pretty much since the day I got here," she confirmed.

"Have you been reading the book of the Paramahamsa?" he asked, "I see you have it with you." She did. It was sticking out of her bag. He didn't wait for an answer, however, and went into a rant about the British, and how they brought the drug culture to India. Rajinder, for his part, was going on about overpriced electronics. Everyone had a different beef. The room was full of loose fragments of sentences, like being at a party or a bar in New York where each person's interest is the most important thing in the world, each person only listening to their own voice. Sophie and I joined the merriment—we talked to ourselves. But pretty soon we were fighting.

"See, he's just like that fucking friend of yours, Damien Dandy, or whatever," I said, in reaction to something she said about my friend Pete Poseur, whom she considered her enemy.

"Damien? Damien's not even my friend, he's yours."

"What are you talking about, I never knew him before I met you."

"Damien says this, Damien says that, that's all you used to say," she said a little too loudly.

"Calm down," someone said. "You Americans are so tense."

"Here, hashish will calm you down." He made an offering.

"No thanks," I said.

"Good for you. Be strong," he said. "Say no to drugs." He himself took a long bubbly hit off the bong.

"Be careful," added the Nameless Man dressed in purple, "because the drug men have scouts and they hang out in the hotels. They turn you into the police for more money."

"You are the police," I said, nodding to Raj. Raj nodded back, smiling, slightly embarrassed.

"Many runaways here, many western people. Western people very often go insane. Their governments and families can't find them. They throw away their passports." The Nameless Man was speaking.

"Or burn them," added Sonny.

"Or sell them."

"Yes. Then we have to find them."

"Throw their passports on the ghats. Or in the Ganges." Sonny seemed to want to keep this subject going.

The Grapefruit Head suddenly had some passports in his hand, "New identity? Price high. But price is little," he said. Everybody laughed. It was a spiritual joke. We figured we'd better laugh with it.

"These are passports found on criminals," Raj said. "Drug dealers."

"What does western lady think?" This was Jada talking with a leer.

"I think you guys are crazy," Sophie said, very obviously looking for an exit.

"She is very wise. Young woman. Very pretty. We are

all truly crazy," said the Nameless Man, moving agitatedly, "Crazy Indians." He was waving his hands in the air and moving closer to us.

I should have been getting nervous from the erratic behavior, but instead I was wondering why no one ever said I was wise. I never claimed to be, and Sophie didn't claim it either, but she didn't mind if people thought she was. Mostly it was a joke to her. And it seemed to be a joke to our new friends as well. But I couldn't tell if they were purposely misunderstanding us in order to patronize her, or if they really were in on the humor.

"Ha ha ha." They laughed like the three Indian stooges. The Grapefruit Head nodded. The guy with the dinner-plate eyes didn't do anything.

"Very wise," someone said again.

"Wise, wise, wise." Everyone was nodding now.

"Alright, alright. Everybody's wise." Sophie was getting freaked out.

"We have a very big problem with prostitution in these cults. Some men pay for woman. Only very beautiful."

"But some not to touch. Only for meditation."

"Yes, that is the case," Rajinder added with a sincerity that seemed fake.

"Yeah right," Sophie said. "Why don't they just use pictures? That's what we do in the States. It's called *porno*." She said the word again, slowly, "poorrnnnoooo."

The men smiled at each other. "Ha ha ha." They looked around the room. Some boy brought out tall plastic glasses with colored water in them. We were supposed to drink the colored water. It was kool-aid. We turned it down—diarrhea.

"Oh look, it's getting late. I want to go." Sophie said, kicking me.

"There is a legend . . .." We cut him off.

"Maybe later," I said. We didn't want to stay for a legend or anything else.

"There's a talk on Kundalini yoga tomorrow. At Kama House. For free."

"Where's that?"

Sonny pulled a card out of a satchel he was wearing and wrote an address on the back. He handed it to me. I gave it a quick glance, then turned it over. It was a card for some place called the Lotus Club, in Bombay. "What's the Lotus Club?" I asked.

"It's a business. I was partner there, still am. I'll tell you when we talk, later."

"Maybe you are feeling alone now, strange land, foreign land," the Nameless Man said.

"You go to the Kama House, house of love," Sonny said in an exaggerated low voice while he made a happy gesture. "You will see many of your own people. Americans. Germans. I think it's good for you."

"Maybe. Well, we've got to go, see you later."

We kept trying to leave but it took awhile. They all wanted us to come to their house and meet their wives. It was nice to think they had wives, but we didn't really want to meet them. Finally, we just left while they were still talking. We figured never to see any of them again, anyway.

*

Sophie had become pretty sick, so we stayed in Benares longer than we normally would have. Then we took a week and went to Bodgaya. It was nice down there, laid back. Monks and tourists lived side by side in a pleasant atmosphere. But it did not last because we had to come back to the Forest of Bliss to get the bus to Nepal. We ended up in a different hotel because the one with the flesh-eating monkeys was full. The festival of the Navratri, the nine nights of the goddesses, had started in Benares, and the goddesses draw a crowd. The crowd did not keep me awake, however. I slept like a dead man who dreams.

*

That night I saw a woman coming out of the upper windows of an old mill in some gothic European village. She was clothed in a white nightdress and robe and she held a candle in her hand whose glow formed a halo. The mill wheel was large with twelve spokes and it turned with menace as she walked a plank just above it. This plank was decayed and shaky and it cracked a little under her weight causing her to drop the candle into the noisy waters below. As the light disappeared, some dogs began to bark in the darkness, and the woman sang, "*I canni stessi accovacciati, abbassan gli occhi, non han latrati. Sol tratto tratto da valle fonda.*" Somehow, I knew these words referred to the center of a great wheel. There was a tiny goddess too, less than the size of a thumb. I also knew that the sound of the mill was actually some kind of motor from which the dogs manufactured their voice. I knew all this for no reason, like an intuition born of intellectual impotence.

*

Two days later it was raining when Sonny came by our new hotel, just to make sure we were alright. He had a different outfit on—part hill station, part humble servant. "Are you alright? You look not well," he said to Sophie. She didn't answer. He went on, "I don't see you at the lecture," he said.

"We didn't go to the lecture. That's why."

(nine)

The Ganges lived and meandered in Shiva's tangled locks long before she flowed upon the plains of India, beaconed as she was to Varanasi, where stand the one thousand phalluses that make up the Forest of Bliss. Thus Varanasi became the ground where Shiva and Parvati made love at the beginning of time. Varanasi is also known as Kashi, the City of Light. Kashi is the eye of wisdom and it swims in the flooded heart of the Goddess like a golden fish.

I always wonder why they don't just go ahead and slice your neck open with that razor. After all, no one would give a damn and they could just shove you off the pier afterwards, along with all the other corpses, candle-canoes and refuse—just one more bloated bodhisattva skin bag on the crowded journey downriver toward perfect humility and non-existence.

The one-eyed man who was shaving me with a pocked and rusted straight razor, read these thoughts in my eyes and laughed. I didn't feel guilty or used though, because if you're going to let someone scrape your face for five rupees you better be ready to have your mind scraped as well, like an unclean dinner plate into the trash before the great wash. And so, with perhaps little time left in this mortal coil, my imagination wandered from metaphysics to sociology, from history to cartography, and, finally, to fantasy. It was the Owl

Creek Incident; it was Pincer Martin all over again—the long deferment—only it was me. In that space between the slip of the barber's blade and the last electric current to my brain I lived a whole life.

I returned to Chicago and married a wealthy woman. Not only was she drop-dead gorgeous but she was the heiress of a vast publishing empire and she loved me unconditionally. She was also humble yet highly energetic. She had French citizenship and we soon moved to a beautiful apartment in the 20th arrondisement of Paris, spending our weekends at her family's chateau in Provence. I grew old and famous and financially secure. At the end, I lay on my death-bed covered with comforters of the finest linen, surrounded by loved ones. I realized I had lived a full life and did not fear death at all. Suddenly, my still stunning wife of forty years started calling me Baba as she hovered above my ragged frame. Her face became elastic, grizzled and weather-burnt. The horrid stench of her breath filled my death parlor until the walls dissolved and I was right back on the banks of the Ganges, face to face with the one-eyed barber with the soapy razor.

"Go on," I said, "slash my throat, I dare you." Or maybe I didn't say that.

The razor was flashing, snickering, and the maniacal barber looked like he might just do what I thought he thought he heard me thinking. Somewhere behind his cocoa brown eyes he must have figured I was pretty funny, or at least desperate. But he rejected my mute plea and asked for money instead. "All done, Baba." I gave him his backshish.

But to backtrack to the previous night: I remembered what Sonny had said about Sophie's weight. I guess I hadn't noticed because the loss was gradual and I was always with her. Unlike the busty stone goddesses chiseled on Indian temples, Sophie's body, which was never "voluptuous" to begin with, had over the course of our travels become downright anorexic. She'd always been both long-waisted and leggy, and it was all held together and suspended by the invisible wires of some frustrated sexual energy.

In any case, she was self-conscious about it. Maybe I wanted to make her feel better, or maybe her frailty made her more attractive to me, but she had become somehow, curiously sexy in her slow vanishing act. At one point, I pursued the impulse, but my attempt to initiate physical engagement caused her to accuse me of finding her weakness attractive. I wondered—could it be true? I also knew, or had read, that life is a disease of matter to begin with, an accident in the far-ago mud, a virus of repetition gone haywire, and so sexuality, in one sense, was merely the sign of physical decay. And, of course, Catholicism promotes this connection between sickly saintliness and sex. That could have something to do with it. Yes, sickness may bring grace, but it is not ultimate knowledge, which means not all sick people are saints, though all saints may be sick people. I was spinning my wheels.

Needless to say the sex didn't happen that day or ever again, but the discussion of the problem carried on into the week as we sought to fill the void. Sophie had become angry with herself and this anger, of course, was turned against me. She said she didn't need me. I took revenge—I said if we went trekking in the mountains she *would* need me, if only to carry all her extra cosmetics. It was supposed to be a joke—a vengeful joke. Instead, it led to an argument about who needed whom. She said she would go to Kathmandu alright, and she would do it alone, a kind of unstated "fuck-you." I said I didn't think she was capable of it. Actually, I knew she was capable of it; I just didn't want to go by myself. Then she threw a glass at me. It was a plastic glass, but still, it's the act that counts. Then I pushed her on the bed and pinned her down. She was red-faced by then and crying, so I let her up.

"Alright, that's it, " she said, "You'll see." Then she lay down on the bed again.

I caught a glimpse of myself in the mirror and realized I needed a shave. I was feeling grubby, and there was an image in my head of an abusive boyfriend in a tank top and a two-day beard growth and, feeling guilty, I wanted to clean it up. "I'll be back later," I said.

"Don't hurry."

*

And now my emergency-escape shave was over and I was clean and smelling like rosewater. It was the sixth night of the Navratri already. We had been staying in Benares specifically for this celebration but Sophie had been too sick to enjoy it, so I decided to do what I wanted to do, alone.

126

I was ready for a stiff one at the bhang stand. "Extra strong," I said. The guy nodded sarcastically. Apparently he knew I couldn't handle it, but being used to arrogant Westerners, he watched me suck it down anyway. I tipped my hat and headed off toward what I thought was the river. Who knows if I ever got there? (I might still be wandering those streets even as I write this, lost in a timeless dream.) My recent brush with death at the barber's had made the colors of the living world a little brighter, a little harsher, and the sounds were louder too. A vast history of want and appetite lay before me. The mouths of babes opened in my direction like great water or wine pots wanting to be fed. Old withered hands, reaching out of nowhere, found me. There were bodies everywhere in various stages of enlightenment, or decay, which, in my newly hyper-engaged state, I realized were different names for the same process.

I passed a man lying in the dirt with a veritable vortex of flies spinning around his rectum—a tornado of fly life shaped like a fecal megaphone and singing like one too. I thought I saw Dorothy's Kansas farmhouse, for a second, swirling around the man's ass. Drawn further on by unseen forces, before I knew it I was in the claustrophobic streets of the old city. Brilliant images collected, then dispersed around me—temples of red stone and painted clay, iron bowls, gold dust and beads. But it wasn't all mystery and misguided Orientalism. Capitalism, too, made a showing. I saw a painting of Krishna driving a Toyota on the wall. Lakshmi was selling Colgate washing powder. Seven women were dragging a small dead donkey corpse down to the dirty river, singing an advertising jingle about biscuits and dairy products. Five men made handprints on a boat. Children twisted colored rags into long sinister ropes for a sinister reason. Some people shunned me, some warned me away from dangerous knowledge, dark streets and secret doors. Others beckoned me to enter their chambers and they signaled their welcome with soft brown, gently waving hands.

I came across numerous folk paintings of Shiva and his consort. Lingam followed lingam. Kali and Krishna and Vishnu and Durga—the gods could be glimpsed standing in courtyards or carved in little rock recesses. Often they were so coated with ointments and flowers that they were unrecognizable. I felt a certain pressure from the fifty-nine Ganeshas that stood in concentric circles at the cardinal points of Kashi city. I felt them spinning around me like a taunting carousel of wronged strangers. Even though Ganesha is best luck, his threshold is odious. I knew I was trying to find that cool fountain in the hidden courtyard that I had stumbled on so many years ago as a child in some exotic dream. But I made many wrong turns in the search. The world seemed to be getting smaller and colder and I could smell the roasting flesh of sacrificial incompetence. I was upriver from the ghats and I could hear the chants and see the fires but they were some distance away, like an overture heard from the opera house while you're stuck outside on the steps.

At the base of the Sindhia ghat there was a Shiva

temple, half sunk in the mud. I popped my head inside as if it were another person's dream. Time was no longer the plastic friend I needed. I came from a world where time was linked to events and their progression; its passage edited itself around the attainment of goals, products, denouements and other literary devices. It went fast because it was never perceived until it was past. But there was another kind of time, more reptilian than ours, less concerned with stimulation, and more related to magnetism, gravity, geologic and/or epic trends—like the opening of prehistoric sunflowers over the long centuries, or the maddening slow buzz of bees over generations of opium cultivation, or the dripping of water in caves and sunken temples.

I suddenly had this feeling that it was water that drove everything—machines and dolls, ecosystems, humans and automatons—and that there was something impious, even pessimistic about knowing this. But I also knew that, due to the unequal distribution of weight and the irregularity of the gravitational field over which water flowed, if water was indeed the Goddess, like Ganga was thought to be, then the insight was a positive and life-giving one, even if it was also demeaning.

There is a legend in which the Goddess gets pregnant from the sound of hummingbird wings, indicating that lust is related to a vague perception of speed, in addition to the death-desire. From the moment you are born you begin to die, they say. Suddenly, I thought I heard Tristan and Isolde's love duet. It sounded like a tug of war between fast passion and slow pulse, amphetamine and heroin, cocaine and thorazine, methadrine and codeine—chemical yin-yang versions of the great momentary now and the fleeting eternity.

Inside the ancient temple, where I thought I heard the sound, I was sure I also caught something from it—a germ-pulse or a brainworm. Whatever it was, some self-initiating circuitry had formed that could easily be mistaken for a divine message—a sound from Shiva himself, or the sound that is Shiva himself, what Sonny had called the Ishvara, or the opening flower of the septic channel of the heart—heard first as music, then words.

"Frank," the voice seemed to say, "carry yourself unto the cremation ground." I wasn't going to fight it at this point.

Oddly, I found myself being drawn towards the ghats, which wasn't that odd because it had been my destination all along—once again I was confusing will with fate. I felt fear, and so I tried to relive certain fights I'd had with Sophie in my mind. Some were remembered fights, others were created at that moment, as a kind of comfort, because fighting was comfort, and familiarity, especially when you don't know what's coming. But you can't fight effectively in reptile time—it's too slow. People looked at me with their strained faces and I returned their strain. I found myself in a parade of men banging on brass pans, playing clarinets and other squealing split-reed sticks. Bodies swathed in red and white silk and tied to bamboo litters were floating through the narrow streets.

The steps surrounding the Manikanika ghat were wide and steep like an amphitheater surrounding a Greek tragedy. Oedipus was there. He said, take a seat. Nearby, wood was being weighed for the pyres. Money changed hands. An argument broke out about who was getting paid and who was paying. It can be confusing: you pay the guards who keep the sadhus and dogs from eating your relatives crisped flesh; you pay them to keep the ragpickers and jewelry thieves away; you pay the sweaty doms in their loincloths to beat the flaming mounds like drums to contain the fire. Death is commerce, of course. I sat and stared at the commerce as black acrid smoke curled into corkscrews and question marks in the air, and I wondered if this was the doubt of the dead or my doubt. Sacred cows nuzzled human ashes at the river's edge. Squatting women in rags raked for relics. I could hear the distant jackals in packs, yelping, and I could see within the flames the black legs of Kali pumping up and down in her dance of hunger and love—the engine of the universe was eating, eating time in an effort to simply maintain itself.

I saw the blackened silhouette of a body on the pyre closest to me, and for a second I thought of Jean d'Arc tied to her martyr's stake sheathed in flames, performing Sati for her Loving Lord. Jean and Ma, the eaters of time. I remembered how Sophie could not watch that old Joan of Arc movie without crying, but that was long ago, back when she used to cry in front of me. And now I had to wonder if that empathy, over the course of our relationship, had infected me. Was it transferred to me in a trick one night? Because now I was the one who often wept, while she kept a straight face. This was an odd development in our relationship.

Then, as if in answer to the unasked question, I saw in slow motion a burning bone fly up, like a plane in the flame. Then a log rolled off its pyre, and it seemed as if the overture in my head were reaching some kind of climax. When the water in the dead brain turns to gas, the skull explodes like some slow prophetic popcorn kernel forming the soft cloud-shape of the supposed soul as it leaves the pyre. You don't always hear it, but you *can* still enjoy the sweet smell and the ancient memory of cannibalism implied in the roast. Sometimes it doesn't happen by itself, and the skull must be broken with a bamboo stick (this is called kapal kriya), otherwise the soul simply remains at the bottom of the bag, unpopped. I was thinking silly thoughts. The music continued to swell. An aria broke out. I tried to pinpoint the source. At the same moment the chief mourner tried to perform kapal kriya, but missed—the unpopped skull bounced off the pyre and rolled toward my feet, emitting a hiss of steam, black smoke and yellow flame. The bone jaws began working, if awkwardly, striving to fight the coming inertia by vocal means. I couldn't quite make it out, but it did sound a lot like the German tongue, which I found discomforting given the subcontinental location. Indeed, it seemed the skull was singing: *"Die Wunde? Wo? LaSS sie mich heilen! DaSS wonnig und hehr die Nacht wir teilen; nicht as der Wunde, an der Wunde stirb mir nicht: uns beiden vereint erlosche das Lebenslicht!"* This apparently means that the gross anatman, infected with appetite, will leak at the seams.

*

Now I'm no Calvinist, but I do like signs. Signs and symbols are like traffic cops at a crime scene—they give us a reason to move along. Thinking back, perhaps it was that Wagnerian smoking skull that served as my clue. I interpreted the voice as a call to action. True, things hadn't been going well between Sophie and I. A lot of old arguments kept cropping up. Inconsistencies. Incompatibilities. Inaccuracies. Besides I just couldn't stand the nagging anymore. Not with everything else I had to contend with. I couldn't take being the source of everything that went wrong. Originally the arguing was fun, mythic, adventurous, even creative. But that creativity eventually exposed all that was irreconcilable between us.

Ultimately I knew her pessimistic optimism contrasted drastically with my optimistic pessimism and this dynamic would be the death of "us." I pretended I could take it all with a grain of salt. Yes, I thought, she could get the train back to Bombay and fly home for all I cared. Indeed, I began to think this was the best solution. And it would be *my* decision, not hers. I would then be free to flirt with the beautiful Indian women who were utterly inaccessible to me. That would indeed be a sweet torture worth abandoning the future for. I

133

once said that nothing less than total devotion could be called love and not laughed at. Sophie didn't agree. I was greatly relieved at the time. Now a ball of lead formed in my gut. It was over, I thought. I realized, of course, that I could only have that thought because I was not really committed to the ending. Suddenly, I was in a race against time. It was dark and I was still high from the bhang, but I took all the right turns in the labyrinth of inner Kashi, and in the name of love I made it home, though I am not sure how long it took.

The hotel clerk gave me a funny look. "Mr. Frank," he said. "You leave already."

"No."

"Yes, you leave."

He had a conversation with his friend, and then they snickered. "Okay, okay."

"Quite an argument, eh Baba?" he said.

"Who? Me? Her?"

"Yes. Memsaab."

I had a headache. And I was experiencing a thirst unlike anything I had ever known. George Jones was on the radio. It was a song about drinking and lost love. "Have a drink," George said, "Drink to lost love." The hotel desk guy smiled. "You don't look well," he said, "Have a drink of water." Despite the incongruity of George Jones on a Varanasi radio station, classic country western songs had never let me down in the past. And since I couldn't remember my room number, I needed to stall for time. I made a move to get that drink from the clay pot of water in the lobby. "No.

No." The desk clerk said, "No good for you. Here." His friend brought out a glass of water for me. "Filtered water," he said. Somehow, I was sure it was. The cool, clear liquid represented everything that was cleansing, and so I took a long purifying drink.

I went up to my room and it was true—she was gone. George was still singing downstairs.

Okay, things had been getting worse between us, but I didn't think she would just move out. But hadn't I been thinking of leaving her just a few minutes ago? Maybe I was mad because she beat me to it. But I was getting way ahead of myself. I wasn't even sure I *was* mad yet, much less that she was gone. A number of her things were still in the room. There was no note.

Who could say where the turning point lay. Or if there even was one. I also had the nagging feeling that Sonny Valentine was involved—that somehow he had influenced or aided her. But what if Sonny wasn't the hustler I thought he was? Maybe he was a stand-up guy. But that didn't make sense, because I knew he *was* a hustler. But who was she arguing with? And did it matter? I knew it was over, I'd known it for a long time, and it was possibly for no other reason than the complete impossibility of ever knowing anyone. And yet it went on.

*

I was overcome with tiredness, as I often am when facing crisis. I lay back on the bed to nap and in my sleep I saw us together again, Sophie and I, copulating on a funeral pyre in some operatic expression of our mutual distrust—two charred screaming figures still going for the brilliance. And there were two singing streams, one of butter and one of blood, surrounding the island on which we would die. A naked man stood guarding the stream of blood with a club. But the stream of butter needed no guard, for it was born from the sacrificial spoon of oblation and true knowledge. Thus out of that butter river rose the men of gold, and they drew up all our squandered human desire in their golden bowls and offered it back to us. *"Ganz ohne Huld meiner Leidens-Schuld?"* the martyred woman beneath me asked at the climactic moment. I awoke briefly to the sound of the flesh-eating monkeys cackling on the balcony. I had this crazy idea they had come all the way from the temple of Durga just to punish me, because they were hungry for the vagrant heart of Frank Payne. But they weren't going to get any today. The store of the fleshy tablet of Frank's heart was closed for renovations. Frank was on vacation in a burning dream.

(ten)

Kali's tongue is like an inside-out vagina exuding itself upon the world, asking to be penetrated by all surfaces. Ramakrishna wanted to know the hunger of Kali and so he would taste what the dogs tasted—rotten meat, dirty water, feces and decay. In this way he would frolic shamelessly, comprehending a scale beyond good and evil, where the impure and the pure are the same and all experience takes place in a kind of transcendental wetness, a sexual sweat, like the primitive salt sea of our bacterial birth.

There is an essential yogi exercise in which the adept expels yards of his own entrails in order to wash them in warm salt water. Supposedly it enervates the senses like a strong cup of coffee in the morning. In a similar manner, Kali extends her tongue and tastes the world in all its filth and glory. To eat is also to embrace. The amoebae embraces food by forming a foot, or tongue of jelly, surrounding the minuscule particle, in the same manner that leukocytes surround a morsel of infection in human blood.

Bags of fluid, born over ten billion years ago in the world's primal slime, still live today in sewer water, in clay pots, and on the thin skin of humidity that coats the silverware in subcontinental restaurants. They get inside you, or rather, you grow around them, and in the process of feeding themselves they liquefy your insides, which then seek release by whatever orifice the body can offer. It's not voluntary but it may be desired, as this vast emptying out can be, and often is, related to religious transfiguration—a certain merging with the stream of life. Clinics and clerics alike claim this kind of suffering may be part of what the Westerner subconsciously seeks on their journey to India, a dissolution of the borders of the imprisoning self, a reintegration with spirit and the world via the mystic method of everyday diarrhea.

That night men and women of the invasive professions gathered around my bed and stuck long needles in my guts, while they talked about the worthlessness of the information they might extract from my pain. They laughed and spat. All the evil physicians of fiction were there: Dr. Benway, Nurse Ratchet, even Victor Frankenstein. Their obsessions became one with those of the parasites within me. But I didn't want their surgery or their condescension, so I visited the toilet to find some peace. After what seemed an hour or two, I tried to stumble back to my room. I failed. I crawled to the toilet again, a prisoner of my newly cellular self, not to mention the thrown-open portals of my incontinent body.

Sickness reduces us to a set of basic but profound sensations, they say. In certain heightened states every hair begins to tingle. And so it was with me. My flesh ran both hot and cold. I could feel the exquisite cool tiles and stone and I tried to incorporate the feeling. I tried to appreciate every little grain of dirt as it rolled across my skin. Every subtle odor seemed like a storm.

I extended my own mouth to the cold floor in an effort to re-swallow my stomach, which was out there somewhere, slowly crawling with great gravitas across the tiles. My colon too was laid bare for all to see; you could have photographed my colon, stomped on it, licked it clean like a drunken celebrity licking the stones of Hollywood Boulevard. I could have interpreted the humiliation as a transformation of my individual wave-form back into the ocean of infinite consciousness. I didn't.

It was in such an indecisive state that I was discovered on that toilet stall floor early the next morning by the hotel manager, asking if I was alright. His skin was the color of a coconut husk and his head was huge with stored semen. But I was curled in a puddle, brought low by some little circle in my blood. So who was I to comment on his self-presentation?

The next couple of days I lived in a Paul Bowles nightmare. I remembered vaguely the approach of faces, voices making mysterious plans, and a strain of horn music twisted into a sinuous death chantey winding through the tawdry tourist hotel halls, and in and out of the mouths of fellow sufferers, cousin dreamers and brother evacuees lined up couches, cots and toilet bowls, the whole defecating West. Large cockroaches clung to my toes like science-fiction telephone linemen, chewing the stale skin of my cuticles, fattening themselves on my physical decay. If I had the strength to kick them off, I would do so, and I would then hear the "thunk" as their chubby green-blooded bellies hit the floor. Through a fog somebody handed me pills and

I ate them. Somebody brought me cups of tea and I drank them. I slept, fitfully.

I believe it was the ninth night of the Navratri when I sensed the footsteps in my room and the amplified sound of saliva dripping on the stone floor, and then a flash of something blue and beautiful—a ghost of a boy who is like a girl—and this was followed by blue flute music and hissing steel. He/she told no story, nor was there a voice I could describe, except to say that it surrounded me. Sometimes I thought it was meant to trick me—to initiate the kind of arousal one first experiences in early adolescence: the clean cotton underwear, the closed-off cave of young loins, that deep reserve where orchids and dead moss cling to virgin tissues. A conversation took place between us; a conversation that can only take place between the muculent recesses of the unviolated body and the pornographic imagination.

"Remain with me," the child said, "Do not let the world trick you into believing you should be alone."

"But I cannot be alone," I said, not knowing who it was. "I am leaking into everything."

"Remember only that *we* do exist. All of us. But you are waiting not for one of us. *You* are waiting for Nobody."

"I am waiting for no one?" I asked.

"Precisely."

There was a gap. But she/he must have had some soothing effect on me with her blue skirts and her erotic gestures, because the next day I felt better. I even went to the restaurant downstairs and had some biscuits and chai. People in the café were looking at me with something like combined fear and curiosity. I couldn't tell if they felt sorry for me, or if they were disgusted by my appearance. Most likely, they were worried they might end up just like me, for I must have looked rather gaunt and rough around the edges, which I suppose is normal for someone who has been vomiting and shitting like a firehose for six days. Then, through the door, out in the street, I watched some dogs chasing a cart of raw meat down the street and I knew I wasn't quite ready for the solid world, so I went back to bed.

The days continued to pass. People gave me things— more pills and tea, grapes and biscuits, magazines and comics. I read a little bit of Ramakrishna's biography. Sophie had left it behind and I was glad to have it. I learned how the saint passed out so often he virtually lived on the floor like a clam, and there he claimed to be both a vagina and a tongue. Ramakrishna had said the mystical flower of the pure light of consciousness draws its sustenance from the muddy bottom of the world. Defecation and mystical union are merely differing wavelengths of this light. Shame feeds the sublime.

And so I took a lesson from the Great Swan: if India can turn nausea into serenity, perhaps I could use the same cliché to turn Sophie's leaving into peace. Cancer and repression have been related, as have tuberculosis and beatitude. Maybe my dysentery could be seen as a psychological reaction, an attempt to expunge whatever part of my personality had driven Sophie away. I'd never had such a violent reaction to a breakup, so maybe it was a way to get her back, to make Sophie feel sorry for me so she would return. But first she had to actually know about my austerities—I would have to find her and show her how I was capable of suffering *for* her.

*

That night my dream began as a story in a newspaper about anxious flowers. I think it was in Kerala, south of Cochin. I was walking our dog and at some point I let the dog off the leash and followed him into an old-growth forest, where I joined a group of explorers dressed in khaki clothing and wearing welding goggles. This forest was like something out of a 50s movie—*The Lost World* or *Journey to the Beginning of Time*. As we got deeper into it, we began to see amazing giant lotus blossoms on the ground. We noticed that the flower petals were lined with tiny teeth because the plants were carnivorous. The scientists called it the "Lucia de Lammermoor" flower because it was known to attract its prey with Italian music, which could be heard very softly throughout the jungle if you had the proper training. Several flowers around us had already closed up and we could see them churning and digesting the bodies of opera lovers inside.

There was something quaintly apocalyptic about this *selva oscura*—a threat of total psychological enclosure and/or loss of memory. Then I realized the dog was trying to get my attention. He pulled at my sleeve and led me away from my companions to a specific spot deeper in the forest. When we got there, he began to dig, in slow motion. The dog was wagging his tail trying to get me to come over to his hole. When I did, I saw he had unearthed a black figure about a meter tall that was slightly corroded. At first I thought it was one of the Black Virgins that people often find buried in this part of the world. It was believed that long ago such Virgins were planted here like eggs by an ancient race. Then I noticed the statue had a number of arms, and that the face looked very much like Maria Callas. I heard a bell at that moment and saw a large white shining cow pulling a cart towards me through the forest trees. Its whiteness seemed to demand some sort of action on my part, so I took up the statue and placed it into the cart and watched the cow move off down a forest path. I heard the words, "*Mircentur ergo saecula quod angelus fert semina quod aure virgo concepit et cord credens parturit,*" which I interpreted as "Listen up Frank, it's time to wake to the challenge of your new life."

*

A week passed and I learned nothing of Sophie's fate. Blonde Westerners were a dime a dozen in the Forest of Bliss and many disappeared, hooked on the cheap heroin, if not on some charlatan's spiel. Sophie was not the druggy type, but she could get distracted. Her moral center shifted with the false facts of the world. She often claimed that this was my flaw, but it was really hers. I knew she wouldn't be averse to some hashish or a glass of potion with an inappropriate con artist. That whole idea about deranging the senses; she really did believe it. I told her she didn't have the balls to do it. Maybe she took my accusations as a dare—doing something utterly antithetical to her normal behavior. There were plenty of possibilities, but there was only one easy one: Sophie had talked about going to Nepal to see the child goddess, the Kumari Devi. And those other tourists, whom we had talked to, had already left, over a week ago, about the same time she disappeared. So, maybe she went with them. It would make sense.

But if Sophie *did* go to Kathmandu—did I need to follow her? Perhaps she *should* go alone. I wouldn't be respecting her freedom if I made a pest of myself. Sophie was always susceptible to people like Sonny Valentine, who himself was a victim of spiritual drift. But the pressures she created for herself were enough—her skewed mythology of "identity," her subscription to the fashion of "empowerment." All of that thrown into the mixmaster of Eastern mystical hoopla could be disorienting, not to mention her physical deterioration. I should have been more attentive at the time, but it was almost too much to attend to—too many clues, too many bifurcations of the path.

For the first time I noticed that there seemed to be an emptiness inside me that could only be filled by the storm that was her. "I'll go to Nepal myself," I thought, "I'll go there and find her and fix this thing." Perhaps I was crazy, but I wanted to move and my excuse to move was to go further, and, as always, Sophie would be the force that would rouse me to that act.

*

But the long drawn-out days of dysentery had drained me. I was standing on the hotel balcony tentatively eating some fruit, and priming myself for a journey. There were some young Uttar Pradeshi girls on the next rooftop, probably twelve, maybe fourteen years old. Probably married already, or at least promised. They were beautiful, laughing girls, with all the energy of the world in their laughter. We began to trade incomprehensible jokes, pointing at things in the sky and naming them. They kept saying "Flying saucer, flying saucer." The sun was setting. It was the hour of *aarti*, when the gods are praised, and across Benares the devout were ringing bells in front of family altars or burning incense in temple courtyards. An airplane flew overhead. I pointed and said "Kathmandu." They didn't know what I was talking about, so I started playing air guitar—Bob Seeger-style—"I'm going to Kathmandu…." The Indian girls also started playing air guitars. They called me Elvis. The entertainment industry cliché drove the point home and some international bonding took place.

Still, I was starting to grow concerned that too many pop songs were forming the pivotal points of my story. But I went down to the Benares train station anyway and pushed and screamed along with everyone else for a couple of hours until somebody in a cage sold me a ticket to some place I did not recognize. Then I watched a man fall off a crowded commuter train. The guy's limbs got mangled under the wheels and he was writhing around for awhile while a massive argument broke out between about a hundred people in white shirts as they decided what to do. There wasn't really anything they *could* do, so they had to compensate with a lot of vocal effect. This caused a delay.

I got on a train but didn't go very far, and eventually I had to get on a boat to cross another river. I fell asleep on the boat floor. I remember people walking by, kicking me. "Get over it," they seemed to yell. Sometimes I would wake up from my half-sleep only to find myself the center of attention for a small crowd of gawkers. I wondered why they didn't just lay into me with their bamboo sticks and "get it over" for me.

*

I realized that somewhere along the line I had begun to associate my increasing paranoia and my impending fear of persecution and violence with some misbegotten quest for innocence. It didn't make sense at first, so I had to break it down. There was the life Sophie had to offer—the life of discord and unending dialectic. Then there was this fake life, where everything is fine but lonely. There were also the various tortured lives of people I knew: Kathe, Bernadette, Arnaud. Each memory image was a diversion, a path away from the face in the mirror, a path both convoluted and escapist. On top of that, figure in the fact that I didn't really even know Sophie that well, at least according to her.

But then I don't know most people. No one does, no matter how close or intimate they become. I don't even believe "knowing" is really possible; it's only a projection of our own obsessive desires. What I did know was that I was thinking too much and it was making me nervous. "Stop thinking," I thought. Aware of the absurdity of such a statement, I let the fog roll off the river and into my mind.

The boat docked that morning. It was still dark. I asked around for the bus. Somebody pointed to a bus and I got on it. The seats were made out of the same hard planks as the floor of the boat. A woman who looked like a dark Sophie—a Sophie with a nose ring and a purple sari—sat across from me. She seemed nice enough and not at all argumentative. God only knows what her troubles were.

Ten or twelve hours passed. Finally the bus reached Motibari. Instead of paying some rickshaw wallah, I decided to walk. Keep it simple, I thought, reciting in my mind some Eastern aphorism I had once heard or read: "I chop wood, I carry water, I walk to town." Before crossing the border, however, I decided to eat, as I was hungry and needed energy. I was also depleted from my recent week of living expulsively. I should have been suspicious of the long black hairs in the white rice. I should have doubted the dingy grey water that was used to wash the silverware, but I never learned much from experience and it was too late to start learning now.

*

Crossing into Nepal, the entourage of cabbies and rickshaws eventually fell away. Indeed, I was glad to be walking, glad to have left India, glad to be outward bound. It wasn't long, however, before the effects of the recent meal began to make themselves known. I was going to be embarrassed soon if I didn't do something about it. There was nothing around but a thicket of weeds by a pond to the left of the road. It was an ominous large pond in a wooded area, but at least it afforded some privacy. It was there I knew the ecstasy of Ramakrishna yet again, if only briefly. But this time I was in nature, if this could be considered nature. But whorehouses were nature, too, after all, and so were world wars. I decided "nature" was poor comfort.

So there I was, sitting on a stone in the shade. The violent wrenching of my intestinal tract had drained me and I wanted to rest, so I took a stick and began to poke the floating body of what I thought to be a drowned monkey—perhaps a clumsy monkey, fallen from a tree, who would now never breed and spread his clumsy genes to the monkey pool. Then with a slow sickening realization, I saw it was really a red baby, a dead red human baby with its limbs hacked off. The child was encircled in a delicate aura of whitish foam—a halo of decay which contrasted with the septic green pond water, and it made small ripples in that green water because little fish were pecking at it from underneath, causing it to pulse with a hallucinatory rhythm, which, over the infinity of those few seconds, seemed to time itself with the rhythm of my own depleted beating heart.

It was a bright day in the world beyond, and there was plenty of reassuring noise along the roadside. One might even have expected some kind of "Thus Spake Zarathustra" soundtrack to accompany this vision, as if it were a subcontinental, back-alley version of the baby in a bubble that floats in outer space at the end of Stanley Kubrick's "2001," a silent focal point that seemed to draw up and swallow all light and sound, while at the same time offering itself as an odd comfort to the confused traveler. And so it stayed in the back of my mind pulsing like a cold dead planet, repeating what seemed to be the words "Nevermore, Frank Payne," like a mantra, "Nevermore." Perhaps I exaggerate here, but there *was* a certain tenacious Poe-like quality to the visitation, only it wasn't a raven, it was a raw decayed red baby without limbs.

I've seen other things at different periods of my life, things of which I seldom speak, or, of which I have had doubts. Nor can I say how such sights affected me, except perhaps that each acted as a temporal door to a past or a future where, suddenly, and for only a moment, I knew more than I do now or ever will. You can read the travel books, the novels, etc., but the veil always falls away if you let it.

*

The experience of the East is not comprehensible, it is said, except after a total re-education of the senses. It is also said that in the third stage of enlightenment, a tree is once again just a tree and a stone is just a stone. Then again there is definitely a difference between being kicked in the teeth and reading a description of being kicked in the teeth, which is to say that since a finger pointing at the moon is not the moon, my thoughts surrounding this hacked red body were, of course, not the body itself, nor were they manifestations of some buried sacrificial obsession, nor was the body any kind of sign unless I chose to make it so. Still, the question remained: was this red baby lodged in my mind, merely another nothing to which I added the something of my predisposition?

By most accounts I've read, God is merely play. There is no body, no mind—just activity. So I took up my stick and continued to play with the little corpse, a girl, as it turned out, pushing the dead girl around in the water with the stick, pretending she was a ship, a link in the food chain, or the chrysalis of a reborn saint, all the while knowing I wasn't spiritually evolved enough to see her for what she really was. But I did see myself suddenly, for what I really was—both part of it all, and, at the same time, separate from everything, a citizen of the universe and a tourist with a stomach problem in a third-world roadside bower, poking a dead baby in a rank pond with a stick. This was no Wordsworthian rustic pastoral, no "spot of time," but it could very well be that Kubrick-like punctuation point, the final note to the symphony of incongruous images that made up my perceptual life.

And then I heard a voice that seemed to come from the road; it could have been male or female but what I heard was: "Open the book and read." But the only book near me to read was the book of the world itself, and it had nothing appropriate or useful to say. Suddenly my mind snapped and I laughed. The universe was new. It was funny, and it stunk. Everything was the same and different. Not that I had attained satori, or anything even approximating true humility. I think more likely I was just embarrassed—profound embarrassment—our modern version of divine humility. But there wasn't anybody to bear witness.

I quickly rearranged my clothing in the position of the infinite present, a state wherein we are denied our religion of regret. We live in a foam of unknowing, and history is full of people who did the worst they could in order to get God to show a face or intervene—it never happens. The secret door had opened despite me. But whether it was good or bad was a judgment call. What I did know is that I had actually forgotten about Sophie for a moment, and that in itself felt good, kind of like some old bum on a public street must feel, who, having shit in his pants, finally lets go of all fealty to social contracts. He doesn't care about anything or anybody's opinion and he is free. But no such luck for me, because Sophie returned to the theater of my mind with her crooked smile and her black-rimmed glasses and her eyes spinning like chariot wheels asking, "Are you coming or not?"

*

It was, by then, nearly nightfall. The small town I came to was little more than a caravan stop—a bunch of wood-frame hotels surrounding a huge mud lot full of buses and bonfires, an insignificant way-station on the dirt road to nowhere. The hotel desk clerk didn't even comment on my condition. I paid for a bed, then I took a shower with all my clothes on. Then I stood at the window and watched the fires burning in the square amongst the stable of buses. Depression and major dependency were right around the corner. It's true the Kumari Devi of Kathmandu was just a few more days to the north, but somehow I no longer needed to see her.

You're supposed to follow the girl out of the bar after the fight. She's supposed to be standing on the corner crying, waiting to be found. I'd been sick for ten days. If Sophie had wanted to be found she would have left a trail. She didn't. She was on her own now. And in days to come I would look back and think it might have been cowardice and not respect that swayed that decision for me.

Part Three

Reviewers have sometimes described the voice of Maria Callas as a questionable, exasperating vocalism. She was often said to intone like a demi-goddess, and an evil one at that. She has been accused of a torturously high tessitura, of ludicrous tremelos, and of a rasping uncontrolled "spread" that could move from mezza voce velvet to a ringing, often assaultive, dramatic metal. Other critics have described her voice as both organ and weapon, projecting colors, cries, moans and other mottled effects while at the same time producing explosions on the various shores of the characters she played: Medea, Gioconda, Santuzza, Elvira, or Lady Macbeth. It was a grandiose voice, capable of filling, or usurping, the entire opera, overwhelming its clichéd drama with mystical qualities. Her voice has been called the lost secret refound, and a monad vibrating in space like an atom that will not cease emitting energy. Some have likened it to a bullfight or a circus.

(eleven)

Back in Chicago, I holed up a few days alone at the BelRay Hotel. As I sipped from my bottle of Jim Beam and reviewed my recent memories, the neon "hotel" sign pulsed outside, causing a neurological digression that turned into a linguistic digression in my mind: Bel-Ray, RayBel, Bel Ray Me, Red Bay Bee. I blinked and tried to stop the association train, but it was already in my brain and would be, for years.

No one knew I was back in town. I rode around on the subway and I nursed drinks for entire afternoons at the Nisai bar on Sheffield. A group of us used to hang there, since it was right next to Gilles' and Solomon's. No one hung out there anymore; everyone was living out in Wicker Park.

Oddly enough, for a cheap hotel, the BelRay had a phone in the room. The phone rang, loudly, and I ignored it as long as I could. I was feeling pretty good about it too, when suddenly I had a vision of the future. I saw an image of my long-lost daughter out on the empty road of life. She was standing at the only phone booth for a thousand miles in a thunderstorm with a flat tire, transmission trouble, a frightened child in the back seat, and a serial killer only twenty miles down the road and headed her way. The guilt was overwhelming. Then I noticed the boney pink spider of my hand crawl across the desktop.

"Hello."

The other voice was distant at first, like the echo you hear inside a conch shell, a voice muffled by the roar of the miles of undulating twisted phone wire. As the voice came into focus, however, it brightened significantly until it was actually too bright for my state of mind, which wanted darkness.

"Did I wake you?"

I looked at the clock. 11:30 pm. Vague cinematic memories of a distant happy hour at Roscoe's Pumpkinhead Lounge for Hopeless Drunks rolled through my head. That would explain the early bedtime.

"Apparently. Who is this?" I asked, risking embarrassment. Something in her voice hinted that we might have known each other before, in Sodom or Babylon or Brooklyn or Portland.

It was Berny, of course. She tried to act like I'd never left. As anonymous as I tried to be, people had seen me around and it got back to her. The next night I was sitting at Berny's kitchen table. We cracked a fifth. The news went like this. First: Kathe was pregnant and wasn't naming the father. Second: Gilles and Solomon had broken up. Gilles was in California, and he was sick with HIV. Solomon still had the store, at least till the lease ran out. He'd become a paranoid depressive, but, as if in reverse proportion, the store was doing pretty good. Times had changed and a black queen with a mohawk in Newtown was considered a draw. Third: Arnaud had been convicted and would go to Stateville with Gacy, Speck, the Kings, the Unknowns and others. Good Times in Joliet. The insanity plea didn't fly. However, he did get away with unintentional or negligent homicide, or was it "man two?" She couldn't remember. Somehow it all got back to the brainwashing issue and the rough sex.

A lot can happen when you leave town—a few months and everything changes; your old apartment building burns down, minor wars come and go, plagues deplete the population, all while you're pursuing some idea of a life, or a dream, or a dream of a life. Berny and I sort of talked around our dreams for a little bit, but it seemed like a dodge.

"Oh, and by the way where's Sophie?" Berny asked, trying to sound off-handed about it.

"Took you long enough to ask."

"I guess I just figured she was at her folks'."

"I don't actually know where she is. She left me in Varanasi. I thought she might already be back here."

"Well, she's not. Nice song title though—My Baby Left Me in Varanasi." She hummed a few blues lines.

"It's not really funny."

"I know. But . . . she left you! Wow! Not what I expected."

"You're surprised?"

"I guess not. But, what does surprise me is—why aren't you looking for her?"

"I'm not really sure. I thought she might have come back on her own."

"No one's heard from her as far as I know. Hell, I only knew you were back about a week ago."

"Maybe she's at her parents' then, hiding out."

"You haven't called them?"

"I'm afraid to."

"Jeez, Frank. You have to. You *do* know that."

I did know. I also knew they would ask uncomfortable questions: Where? Why? What? When? But I figured they knew her better than me and knew how bullheaded she was, and for once that obstinacy would weigh on my side.

"Call them now, asshole." She handed me her address book, pointing at the booth in the corner.

I handed it back. "Later," I said.

*

They were surprised to hear from me, but I detected some anger under the surprise. And no, she wasn't home. In fact, they hadn't heard from Sophie in about a month and were justifiably worried. Indeed, it would have been a little more than a month since I last saw her. I told them only part of the story, making it sound like a break-up. They admitted she was stubborn, and might walk off like that. But she was also a daughter who kept in touch. She had an obsession with communication. She couldn't keep secrets either. But that's something else. Still, it was odd that no one had heard from her.

Berny called Boggs, who was back. He called some other old friends. Nothing. And yet everybody agreed something like this was inevitable. They couldn't see us getting through a whole trip without some major crisis. But they didn't think she would disappear. I repeated the whole narrative again, spinning it, concentrating only on the negatives—the arguments, the ugly scenes—to make myself look more sympathetic. I told them about Calcutta and Varanasi and Sonny Valentine. They all agreed it was highly suspicious and that we all ought to be worried about it. Then we opened a new bottle.

I changed the subject. "So, tell me again how Arnaud was convicted." I asked, "I'm surprised the case went to trial so quick. Those things usually take years."

"Yeah, I don't know," Marcus said, "But he was like a minor celebrity for awhile. That's probably why."

"Yeah, about a week," Berny added. "Some celebrity."

"Another city council scandal and Arnaud was old news."

It was Marcus Boggs who brought it up that Arnaud might have known this Sonny Valentine character in Portland, or at least Marcus thought it was possible. Arnaud *had* been living there about the same time: "in the 70s, and he talked about that guy on Burnside, remember?" he said, looking around for verification. And then, of course, some of us did start to remember such stories. We were implanting memories in each other with some facility, and, given another hour or so we would all be remembering childhood Satanic cults. Still, Arnaud *had* told his lawyer about a guru-type guy that he met, but neither the lawyer, nor anybody else, took him seriously. I myself never made the connection, or at least I never thought it meant anything. I wasn't sure it did now. One minute it seemed perfectly clear. The next minute it was virtually impossible.

"Hey, so do you think Sophie was maybe kidnapped?"

This started out as a joke, but it turned into serious speculation. I couldn't really imagine it, but I suppose it *was* possible. I remembered some tourists at the Dharma Bum Inn who talked about a woman being carried off in a burlap bag—but that was an Indian urban legend. I had heard stories like it in a couple of different towns. Besides, I couldn't see Sophie in that kind of situation—stuffed in a bag. It was too undignified for her. Obviously, something had happened, but not that.

Over the next few days I said as little as possible, but the rumors grew on their own. A few pegged Sophie as a victim of various charlatans. Some said she might have gotten AIDS over there. I didn't want to think about that. Someone figured she had probably gone to Nepal, but may have gotten lost in the Himalayas; it happened all the time, they said. Another person claimed she had probably become a junky living in a forest outside Bodhgaya, that she weighed ninety pounds and lived with a Dutch flutist. They had read a story in a travel magazine where something like that had happened.

"Christ," I said, it's only been a month, she's probably still traveling around." But I also knew that our visas would have expired by now. But then, they're not that hard to renew.

A lot of this conversation had a jokey quality to it, although I did detect a serious undercurrent, an insinuation perhaps that I had been lacking in my duties as proper boyfriend and caring person. And since I was to blame for every negative thing in Sophie's life anyway, at least according to her, it would be natural for the world in general to take up that particular accusation. Before long I had the reputation of someone who abandons a helpless woman in a bad place. "But she acted on her own," I claimed before my accusers, "I had nothing to do with it."

But it did have something to do with me—I was there. And now I was here and I was uncomfortable with this note of traditionalism and family values that seemed to be creeping into the outlook of my normally anarchic clan. As I looked at them sitting there, I realized their lives had gone on without me. Things had changed, and those changes ruined my faith in my autonomous worldview—that the world has no real existence until I apprehend it. Obviously things do exist despite me or, rather, to spite me.

*

The next day I lay around in my room and worked up a profile of this Sonny Valentine character. I got out my forensic brushes and easel, poured a glass of bourbon and started to paint a revised portrait. I was a little unfocussed, but so was the subject—East, West, curse or boon, half-Manson, half-Moon; Valentine began to seem like one of those medieval monsters made up of many incongruous body parts, a walking, talking fragmentation/redemption epic acted out on the stage of my unresolved psyche. Oddly enough, on the streets of Calcutta, where no one stands out, he did stand out, at least to me, like a moving cubist painting avenging itself on the cynicism of stray Western youth. I could see it. I could even see a weird sexual attraction to it, but not necessarily for Sophie.

Then an odd bit of an old conversation came back to me. I remembered what Sophie had once said about facing your demons, and that, as Berny filled me in, there had even been such an episode in Sophie's early life, a youthful indiscretion with an older man, a supposedly hideous man. So the next day I called Bernadette for reassurance.

"I think it was just her general opinion of men," she said, "that, behind whatever chivalric pose they might assume, they were all hiding an inner sweating, hairy, rutting pig."

I couldn't argue with that. Sophie had never said anything to me about any such episodes, and I would have thought she was making it up anyway. It's also true that if it ever looked like I was starting to believe her, starting to take one of her stories seriously, she always backed off and said it never happened, that she was just kidding, but, of course . . ."What if?"

She said, "What if?" a lot. But I knew her "what-if?" often merged with "could have been," and that could glide subtly into "probably was," which was code for "Don't you wish you knew?" Thus, before you did know, you didn't know. I mean there was an element of doubt that she always encouraged. And she always took everything back, too. Her truth was dependent on reaction. If she thought you were displeased, she might take it back just for that reason. Or then again, maybe if you weren't displeased *enough*, well that was provocation to backpedal. I think she just wanted everyone to know her potential.

Beauty feeds off degradation, she once said, thinking she was quoting Baudelaire. And suddenly I *could* see her giving herself sexually to some pock-marked misogynist with bad breath. It made sense. By forcing the extreme, it made her in some way more aroused, yet more pure—converting the whore back to a virgin, metaphorically speaking. It wasn't animal attraction like some people want to think; the act is not between male and female *per se* but between beauty and its opposite, between vanity and a kind of tragic humility.

*

I called Sophie's parents again a couple weeks later. At this point they were very worried, and they had started going through diplomatic channels as far as they knew how. They had contacted the Indian and the American embassies. No, she had not renewed her visa, but that was normal. To the authorities, it was just another case of a white woman, alienated from her home and family, running away to India. It happened every day, just as Rajinder had said, and there was almost no way to trace them. People often stayed for years without getting their visas renewed. It was hard to control. She could be in Puri or Poona or Pondicherry or Panjim, right now, scrubbing the stained feet of some sick sex freak. Their advice to the parents was to wait it out; when she was tired, she would come home.

There were the other theories, however, mostly psychological explanations that I didn't express in public, the main one being that *I* was, in fact, the kidnapper. It was exactly how Sophie described our relationship anyway, that I had trapped her in a life she didn't want, and so, in the end, if it finally went bad, she could say she had no part in it; it would all be my manipulation of her that made it so.

*

Two months passed. No news. By then I was working at a crummy bookstore job. One day Marcus called. *60 Minutes* was doing a special about prostitution in India. They focused not only on the sale of lower-caste daughters from poor families, but also on several organizations that preyed on Western women. These organizations played sympathetically on the weakness of the traveler's memory, their insecurity, and their hunger for experience, breaking down barriers slowly. It was either Mike or Morley who explained how one drifts into this mindset of subservience in incremental stages, minute shifts in morality played against Christian guilt.

And because the victims were from the West, material indulgence, especially bodily pleasure, was a medium that could be readily disguised as religion. Eventually it was not possible to tell if resistance or submission was the better course.

It began as simple service to a master. Drugs and sexual indulgence were sometimes used. Slowly, the women were introduced to other men who were either friends or masters themselves, a kind of serial mentorship that sped up over time. The women never saw money change hands, and so the slow slide from spirituality into prostitution was not perceived. Doubt was allayed by contextualizing the debauchery as a *positive* loss of self, a renunciation of emotional attachments.

Client demand for western women was high among the Brahmin class and Arab oil men and there was never enough product. Kidnapping existed because the market did. It was rare, but it happened more than people thought. The Indian authorities took payola from the clients. The 60 Minutes crew interviewed people with black bands covering their eyes. Marcus said he heard the name Robert Werther or Ravi Walther, or something like that. He thought it might have been the name Arnaud had mentioned, the guy from Oregon. He wasn't sure though, and neither was I, and it was likely we were looking for something that wasn't there.

It didn't take long before I started to "remember" things I had forgotten, little scenes and conversations: like how I had dropped hints to Sonny of where we would be; or how I purposely delayed my return to the hotel that day, getting high and giving her more time to be kidnapped; or how I purposely drank the bad water, knowing that it would make me sick and I wouldn't be able to track her. I even remembered a wink that Sonny had thrown my way, implicating me in the events to come. I started to have daydreams, or rather, paranoid hallucinations, memories of Sonny as a ubiquitous Clare Quilty character popping up everywhere in our travels. I never saw him, but I felt he was around, following me, retroactively poking his head into scenes where he didn't belong.

He was there in Bodhgaya, writing in his notebook, watching Sophie from a safe distance. I could swear I remembered seeing him, taking pictures in Bubaneshwar, too. Even in Madurai, I was sure he was watching us from the crowd. He must have picked up on us in Goa—that would make sense—Goa, that land of low-hanging fruit. I could see him hustling his victims there, fresh off the planes from Europe and America. Getting naked, getting high. He was probably in the Benares hotel that night, putting Ganges water in a glass for me to drink, thus gaining a few days on me. That might explain my hallucinations. The hotel clerks had to be in on it, too. That's why they insisted on switching the water.

*

One night I dreamed I was in St. Sulpice cathedral, and there was a door in the back that led to a stairwell that went down into the Parisian sewers. I was looking in the water at the dark forms that crisscrossed beneath me. I thought they were the backs of sewer whales but someone said they were narwhals, which I understood to mean "never well." I was suddenly swimming with these creatures, and they led me to an underwater cave. At some point it became apparent I had entered a vast plumbing system. Eventually I could see a light ahead which grew in size until I realized I had come to an opening. I reached up out of the water and grabbed the white porcelain rim that appeared like a halo and pulled myself out of a fancy toilet in a luxuriously appointed bathroom. When I looked in the mirror I saw that my skin had turned red, which might have been due to the rusty water or to the blood of the sacrifices being carried out on the sewer banks below the building.

Then I left the bathroom and climbed a long series of steps, emerging in a kitchen. I could distinctly hear singing and I tried to follow it but was often sidetracked, sometimes for weeks at a time, in other people's stories—mysteries, romances, action/adventures—indeed, all I had to do was look through a keyhole and I would be transformed. It occurred to me that it was a house of memories and the singing voice was coming from deep in the center of the memories, and I could even feel the house turning around me, as if everything was being drawn toward that center.

Finally, I came to a drawing room. There was no one around but there was a table with a small, flat, very old TV screen with nothing on it but static. This TV was the only black and white thing in the otherwise very plush surroundings of red velvet curtains and tapestries and grotesque stone and woodwork to which the TV stood as an opposing force—the seduction and the loss. There was a red velvet armchair in front of the screen and so I sat down to watch the static. Over time I noticed an image struggling to appear from the static. A face would reform only to *unform* again. Sometimes I would see the vague outline of a woman in what seemed a stained white gown, dancing. "*Straniero! Gli enigmi sono tre, la morte e una,*" she sang. "Let it all happen. After all, what do you have to lose, Frank?"

I didn't know.

"Nothing, nothing is ever lost," she answered for me as she flicked open a switchblade.

This seemed like a threat. I was trying to wake up. I thought I could force it.

*

The next day I got a call from Eddie Walker, Sophie's dad. They'd received a letter. She hadn't said where she was, but the postmark was Bombay. The letter reassured them that she was alright and that they shouldn't worry or try to find her and that they should wire some money to a certain Banco del Indio on Sri Bhagwan Boulevard. She mentioned nothing about coming home. Ed asked me if I knew anyone in Bombay. They wanted to call the police. I also think they wanted me to go and find her. I think they figured I owed them.

(twelve)

It was said that Ramakrishna needed only to look upon a tree and by association he was reminded of the aesthetic hermitages of the forest saints. The color of a peacock's neck called to mind for him the skin of his cosmic lover. Perhaps love and anxiety are the same for such a god. Perhaps they are the same as god. At least one leads to another. I thought back over the last several days, trying to add narrative structure to what seemed like random events; posing questions meant to do just that. Was it coincidence that an Egypt Air to Bombay would have a last-minute empty seat? Was it coincidence that Solomon came across a lucrative auction gig and volunteered to loan me some bread without my even having to beg? Do these things matter in the final interpretation? Is there a hub to this thing? Or is it just rolling—like an empty rim?

I remember passing the usual gauntlet of Chicago street scenes on my way to the train, and I felt somehow as if they had been laid out for me like a table of film stills: scenes of mental pestilence and disorientation, child abuse and parental disrespect. The people were confused, bitter, fighting over, and against each other. Their leaders had failed them, and there was nothing on the horizon to hope for. It was my mission to prove the value of human bonds, and the extent that two people might go to preserve them. I would restore faith to this age of cynicism, if only in my own movie version.

*

I stopped at the Berghoff, Terminal 2A, for a corned beef sandwich with sauerkraut and a beer. As the lager washed my palate, I had a vision of Lord Ganesha, dancing his dance of mad chance, ever the elephant-headed guardian of the thresholds of space/time. I also saw Sonny Valentine. He was sitting behind a big oak desk under a ceiling fan, laughing maniacally. I could see the syllables "ha ha ha" spelled out in a cartoon font floating in the air.

What if Sonny's game was really mine? What if I had manufactured the game in order to free myself of responsibility for my rather gameless life? But the doubt created a space and deceit rushed in to fill it. As Sophie so often said—passivity is action. Indeed it is. And then I saw the woman herself, her pale paper-thin form glowing moon-white on a backdrop of tropical foliage. I heard her voice as she asked, "Frank, what if I left you? You'd miss me, you know."

It's only the flood of memories that holds our world together. But memories have no basis in fact, and, on top of that, I wasn't even sure the memories were really mine, even though they occupied *my* mind. Maybe it was fiction. However, the threat of fiction never stopped me before—I always went with it as a more fulfilling path. I saw myself as a detective on *The Case of Vague Despair*. Admittedly, it was a script for which I wasn't prepared. I'd entered my own story as a votive character, an agent, an actor. It had nothing to do with

Sophie at all. But I had another problem; I wasn't sure I actually *was* doing it, or doing anything, for that matter, because I didn't remember making any decision, I was just sort of being carried along. It's an old problem.

*

I was in row 37, aisle seat, left side facing the cockpit. I always take the aisle seat because of my knee pain. Besides I'm claustrophobic. The guy sitting next to me was reading *Ulysses*. I figured that meant I wouldn't have to talk to him. I was wrong. Apparently he was a professor of "Modernism and its Discontents"—from some college in the West. He was going to a conference about the relationship between post-colonialism, the fragmentation of the psyche and the lack of meaning in media culture. And he was happy to talk to me about it. The flight to India is long.

While Professor Modernism rambled on, I went over some fun facts concerning my situation. If Sophie really had hooked up with Sonny, it was unlikely she would have stayed for long. She was many things, but she was not gullible. And I couldn't see her strung-out in some run-down brothel either—she wasn't the type. But then again maybe that's exactly the point; she knew the implications all along and went with it anyway. It was defiance, disruption, and, as Bernadette had said, Sophie would go against her own principles to spite others, even if she was the worse for it. Somehow I couldn't buy it, though.

There was, of course, always the chance that Sonny Valentine had nothing to do with any prostitution ring, fictional or otherwise. Maybe I was awkwardly merging separate strains of fantasy in a desperate attempt to justify my new self-image—part Marlowe, part Father O'Malley. It's also possible Sophie was simply bored with me, and since I didn't want to acknowledge that, I continued to elaborate this fictional crime scenario. But that was a dangerous path, and if I kept going I might reach the further conclusion that I had made up my whole life simply to avoid boring myself. Or, maybe there was some other secret trauma, some other secret door. But that was for the shrinks to figure and the saints to capitalize on. Maybe I had nothing to do with it at all. Truth is, I wanted to think I had some influence on her life, and so it's possible I created a scenario where I could be guilty of abusing that influence, if only to prove its existence. After all, you can't abuse something you don't have.

Finally, the motion-sickness pills kicked in and I was asleep.

*

In the dream I am standing in a forest filled with Christmas tree lights. The camera of the dream lens zooms in, but there is no sound. Instead there is the interior of a gothic cathedral. I'm standing at the door awaiting an invitation. A jester appears out of nowhere, juggling soft leather balls of different colors. I follow him through various halls and chambers until we arrive at an oversized corroded metal door. Its hinges make a certain symphonic sound as it opens—an overture of opening, as it were. Behind the door, taped to a moldy brick wall, is a tiny portrait of a blonde woman clothed with the sun. I notice the voice echoing through the architecture around the apse, and across the vaults, but I can pick up only a few words, *"Il dolce suono, mi culpi di tua voce. Ah quella voce m'e qui nel cor discesa."* Then I realize it's the stewardess shaking my arm. "Sir, You have to fasten your seat belt—we'll be landing in Sahar International in a few minutes."

*

Out in front of the arrivals terminal, some procurer seemed very interested in getting me to take a particular bus, and when I did, I realized it was almost an exact replay of the first time I had entered Bombay. I even think the bus driver was the same guy. He nodded to me as if he knew everything about me—my crime, my taste in women, my hat size, my need for redemption. He also knew it was futile—that I would never find the woman, and that like every other dude who came to India on a private quest-narrative, the only lesson I would learn was: you can travel a long way to find out that no one loves you in a foreign land.

As the bus barreled along we passed the same garbage heaps of humanity, the same pleading voices seeming to rise up from the crowd, the same prayer

flags of poverty, chewed-up and eaten by moths and lo-
custs, hanging from the same fences and lamp-posts
of the scrap lumber and sheet steel shanty-towns. But
who was I to make demands on reality? Eternal return
may well be just another term for entropy, or better yet,
stagnation. You think there is an interval in between
but it's only in your head. Then you wake up one day to
find nothing has happened at all.

We arrived at Victoria Terminus, that elaborate station built over the ancient temple of Mumbadevi. "Get
off the bus," the driver said. I got off his bus and got on
another one headed down to Coloba where I found a
hotel, and it was the same damn hotel—The Seafoam.
Not exactly the same room, but close enough. The
same workers were still outside too, rolling wheelbar-
rows of bricks and concrete over bamboo scaffolds. The
port was still simmering like a pool of tepid soup. The
Gateway to India, symbol of imperial power, had not
fallen. The Elephanta caves on the nearby island still
offered sculptures depicting the sexual practices of the
gods to various repressed tourists.

*

It stormed that night in Bombay and I dreamed of
waking up in bed in my apartment in Chicago, circa
1985. I would often get up in the middle of the night
and go to the kitchen for something to eat—a problem
with my blood sugar no doubt. The floor was done in
checkered tile and the kitchen cupboards were painted

a dark shade of melon. It was an old apartment and there were many layers of paint that could be seen at the chipped edges of door and window frames. It was when I reached into the cupboard to get a package of biscuits, that I saw her—a small doll-sized image perched on the wall-papered shelf, going through a series of theatrical gestures, flickering like a bad light bulb in a thunderstorm, threatening to disappear. I saw her mouth move for a moment, her lips like a cut fig: "*Zu End' ihr Gram : seine Mutter ist tot. Dich grusset Wonne und Heil zumal.*" For that moment I thought I was free, but the sound flickered and caught in the same manner that the image did. There was something almost intolerably sad about the woman's inability to express herself. Then I remembered there was a pull-chain just outside the cupboard and so I reached for it thinking I could turn the doll off and that maybe she would thank me in some alternative universe for her peace. The first happened, the second never did.

*

I took a familiar bus from Ghandi Pradesh Marg. I jumped off the bus and walked down familiar streets. Not much had changed in the intervening period of time, or if it had, I probably misremembered it. I seemed to be on a movie set, and the plot of the script was my own return to the scene of the primal crime. The young whores all knew that I was seeking redemption and that I would fail. Perhaps this was not something that each woman or girl knew in particular, but that they knew collectively, just as they also knew that in order to achieve this dream, I would submit to the humiliation spectacle they were happy to provide. India is a communal place by necessity—everybody is participating in your quest, either as bait, as provocateur, or as mere distraction.

The business card was my ticket, the one Sonny had given me a few months earlier: *Lotus Club*, Paradise Garden, No. 73, Falkland 13. I rang. A middle-class, middle-aged woman, slightly rotund, in the usual sari get-up, came to greet me at the top of the steps. I showed her the card. I took a chance. "Sonny sent me," I said. A look of disapproval seemed to shade her face.

"You come from Sonny?" She didn't pay much attention to the card.

"Yes."

"When did you last see him?"

I said nine months.

"Not long enough." She handed the card back.

"I think I'm ready," I said.

"And how would I know that?"

I showed American dollars.

"So, do you know what we do here?"

I pretended that I did.

She called herself Bhairavi—no last name. She led me into a small living room/office, sat me down and gave me a talk while rolling a one-thousand rupee note in her stained fingers. A small songbird twittered in a gold cage above her desk. She said her specialty was developing girls and boys professionally for certain "rituals." She made the point that they were not slaves; their minds were their own. She groomed them and made sure they understood exactly how to conduct themselves—mechanically at least. It was a true art—this she guaranteed. Along with the overcoming of any sexual self-identity, was the suppression of the desire for money. Both were to be postponed. There was no quota, no expected resolution, no running clock. Of course proper compensation was expected, which she was sure I was good for. No amount would be explicitly stated, but if insufficient I would be led to understand. She nodded to the two silent, rather burly shadows just outside the door. She made it clear neither she, nor the establishment, bore any responsibility if I did not succeed.

I asked for an older woman, pale or light-skinned, figuring this would be understood as code. Bhairavi looked at me with suspicion, then added that I was not to make a choice; all the girls were equal in terms of skill, and any "choice" on my part would demean the process through desire or some other emotional factor.

Did I agree?

I said I did. I was an apt pupil.

I was then shown to another room, "the grove," as she called it. The grove was light and painted in a pastel rose shade. There were jars of ointments, spiced oils and silver bowls of incense. The swan designs of the lace curtains cast shadows on the wall, and a slight breeze would make the swans dance. The sheets were clean and colorful, if slightly threadbare. A roach the size of a human fist crawled across the floor, fat and satiated. Behind the mask of jasmine one could detect a slight fecal smell, along with soapy bath water, cinnamon, something medicinal and something perfumed. That's why perfume was invented, I surmised—it helped the new humans get through the sex act without retching. Defecation and mystical union may well be different faces of Eve, so to speak—but there are limits.

I figured this to be a house of trial as opposed to pleasure, although I was not quite sure what to expect, or if there was any real difference. I waited a few minutes by myself, then the girl was brought in. She was introduced as Kamala Rati. I don't know why she needed a name. At first I thought she might be Nepalese, for no particular reason, but with the cosmetics and the costume it was difficult to tell. She seemed almost mannequin-like, albeit with a certain tragic resignation. She had large kohl encircled root-beer eyes, eyes the color of Midwestern slough water stained by autumn leaves. Her brows were artful and her face was lightly powdered to set the eyes off. She wore a red jewel for a bindi, some kind of beaded silver head-dress, and a variety of bangles and anklets. She had a slim but square, short-waisted body covered with red garments of light linen or gauze. All in all, she was a child goddess of a heart-breaking beauty that was both painful and sorrowful to see, tempered as it was by our brutal reality.

"She won't speak at first," Bhairavi said. "She will approach you to begin, and remember, you must not touch her. She will touch you."

Throughout all this, Kamala sat stone-still, her expression flickering between brain-dead stupidity and mystical intelligence—again, a boundary I was not sure really existed. Her eyes moved with a kind of Kathakali-esque mechanical motion, but languorously, like a relaxed cat eyeballing the room for a mouse. I felt no curiosity on her part, but I did vicariously feel the pain of the muscles that moved those eyes, and my own eyes began to imitate that pain.

I can think, I can wait, I thought. "Will I know what she wants?" I asked.

"It is not she who wants. Yet it will only be she who acts," Bhairavi said. "You, however, must refrain in every way. If you find you are unable to contain yourself—well, many men say it helps to visualize their mothers or some other close family relative, a sister or cousin, or to think of old wounds, sickness, or some past humiliating event. There are obvious reasons why any of these might work. But keep in mind, distraction is contrary to the point."

Kamala was looking at me now with a soft intensity. "How old is she?" I asked.

Bhairavi hesitated. "Seventeen. Older for you," she said.

A young seventeen, I thought. Maybe fourteen.

I started forming one of those lists in my mind, a practice that seemed to plague me all my life. I always believed the repetition of motifs could be a binding and fortifying thing; we can applaud the fact that there is continuity and that the world seems to organize itself around important themes. Some might see in these patterns proof of higher intelligence. I did not. Still, the girl's age was one of those themes. The Sufi mystic Ibn Abi, after all, was obsessed with a fourteen-year-old. The poet, Novallis, was engaged to Sophie von Kuhn when she was fourteen. Humbert Humbert fell in love when he was fourteen, to the fourteen-year old Annabel Leigh. Dante's Beatrice was fourteen when she died. Joan of Arc was fourteen when she first heard the voices of the angels. Joseph married Our Lady when she was just fourteen. Jerry Lee Lewis married his fourteen-year old cousin Myra Gale Brown. Isolde was fourteen when she met Tristan. Mann's Tadeus was fourteen, as was Salome when she demanded Jokanan's head on a platter. All this historical fourteen-year-old lust and spirit helped to allay my guilt and justify my existence for the time being. I began to feel better.

Obviously, I'm stretching the truth of these fictions to accord with my obsession, or at least with my immediate situation. It's just as likely that many of these characters were older, or younger. I myself once fell for a girl who kept canaries. I believe she was fourteen when she went insane. It's funny that it was only then, confronted with the body of Kamala Rati in a Bombay bordello, that I remembered how much the Canary Girl looked like Sophie Walker/Wagner. She wore the same glasses, she had the same carriage and style. I could almost say she was an omen, but it's only aftersight that makes an omen seem so.

I suppose one could say fourteen, which is at the precipice of puberty, is also the outer edge of the pedophile's window of obsession. I'm not trying to justify pedophilia here, only to meditate on its demonic nature, "to certain bewitched travelers . . . you had to be an artist or a madman, or a creature of infinite melancholy," as Monsieur Humbert once put it, and so I steal his words. It is also significant because Ramakrishna himself worshipped Kali in the body of a fourteen-year-old girl, and when he died it was said his spine was hot from the spiritual energy coursing through it.

I was experiencing some of that coursing spirituality myself when I realized that Bhairavi had left the room. Kamala was standing in front of me with her left foot placed on my right foot—some kind of sexual gesture, I guessed. Then she took the sleeve of my shirt in her small hand and led me to a table where she poured some light rose-colored liquid into a glass. She made the motion of drinking. I did. It was a slightly sweet, rose flavor. Then she took my hands and rubbed them, using some kind of powder. I had not realized before how much my knuckle-bones had ached all my life, and how much they needed exactly this attention. Then there were two small silver saucers, one with a light yellow paste, the other with a deep red paste. These pastes were rather dry but she rubbed them on my forehead and temples anyway and they stuck. She then led me back to the middle of the room, and left me standing there while she moved about quietly lighting candles, placing small bowls and jars where she would need them, all the while softly talking in a language I could not understand. But it was a melodious language, even chime-like. I didn't know if it was actually addressed to me or not.

I was aware of various sounds, as this room communicated with other rooms. The walls were thin and I thought I could hear the sighs and moans of sexual activity from other areas of the building, and I had the odd idea that all this sensual vocalization was being piped in somehow, or maybe there was a tape recording somewhere playing these lovemaking sounds. I could also hear the noise of people washing pans and talking, but it was distant.

I felt shame, as she was so young and I was really old. I remembered what Sonny had said though: "Everyone is perverse, my friend, you just have to make it work for you," or something to that effect. So I prayed to the spirit of Ramakrishna for a perverse strength. I knew the saint had exposed himself to prostitutes, that he let himself be teased to the edge of physical release, that he doted on the pearl resulting from his denied ecstasy, and that he treasured it, worshipped it, tried to funnel the temporal pleasure it promised into his head where it could expand for eternity. Somehow, however, the Ramakrishna method was not working for me on this day.

Kamala then lay upon the bed and posed—not the standard porno stuff, of course, but something both girlish and naïve, ritualistic and forbidden. The swan curtains of the brothel windows, their shadows falling across her body, re-enacted, in gestures both violent and tender, the ancient legend of Herculean conception. It was Leda and the Swan all over again, in a Bombay back room. Was I being asked to participate in the myth? Perhaps the elusive egg that lived in this girl's body was acting as a magnet for some divinity riding on this breeze, a quality I was desperately trying to channel to my head to get the proper effect.

But I had no training, and fell into habitual imagery, as what unfolded in my mind was my own lotus blossom of American pathology. Perhaps it was the swan curtains or the color scheme or the cracked wall paint that caused it, but my vision of transcendent eroticism turned into some kind of Speck/Aquino tableau, with the killer going for the glory on the naked body of the Filipino nurse. Suddenly I was at the crossroads making a deal with Jack Scratch himself. But then, into my fog, I felt a child's hand reach, pulling me back from this abyss of maya—it was Kamala. Her eyes, like those of Parvati herself, sparkled with nothing less than the intention to destroy my will, my hard-won asceticism, and to convince me that the world desperately needed our coupling, if merely to continue to exist, and I could then feel every electric impulse within me straining out, seeking a ground in her body.

Her skill was one of pressure, of proximity, and a kind of erotic pointillism. Alternately supple as a jaguar or taut as a hunter's bow-string, she was always present exactly at the precipice of an immense carnality, as her eyes and voice, the fluid arcane hand dance she performed in waves, her mumbled song from some far ancient realm, all served to carry me off until I was lost in vast undefined space—a grainy place without color, an ocean without marker. And yet there was a vibration which sort of kept me afloat and I had the odd vision of cosmic vocal chords, and something telling me that I ought to "*kiss* the throat," but I could not. "Kiss the throat," it said again.

Indeed, I was not sure if I was up to the master's journey. At least not today. And yet here I was. Some resolution was being demanded. My defenses were failing. It was then that Sophie's memory showed up to save me. She had chosen this moment to intervene, to deflate the intention. She accused me of infantilizing her and this seemed an odd accusation considering my circumstances. I would have expected something more like "neglect" or "disinterest." But infantilization? Only Sophie would think this. Perhaps it had something to do with the possibility that I projected some aspect of Sophie into this situation, though I could deny it. But how could I tell Sophie that, in this moment, I couldn't even remember what she looked like, that there were too many masks, too many veils? And how could I tell Sophie that my failure to picture her could be interpreted as a kind of success, and that she should be pleased that no association between her and the young prostitute was made? But, of course, if I said any of these things I would be cutting my own throat. Maybe this act of masochistic continence did nothing but to disprove my affection for her after all.

The argument went on in my head for a while until I realized that Kamala had abandoned our duet and sat there alone and stoic. I don't know how much time had already passed—more than an hour, guessing by the shadows. And I would have lain there for a good time longer, but I could tell by the movement behind curtains that I needed to leave. And so I got dressed. Had I won or lost? Kamala looked bored, which for some reason bothered me. I left the room and paid Bhairavi. She did not ask after my success, and I didn't ask after Sonny either, although I did notice the curled serpents tattooed on her wrists, which she seemed intent on my seeing.

*

I didn't think about it again until I stopped in the Rava Lounge for a beer. I desperately needed some kind of satisfaction, and some cold satisfaction at that. The hopelessness of the situation was overwhelming. I knew I would be returning to the States soon. Maybe I had never really expected to find Sophie, and so I didn't really try. I could have just stayed home, but the narrative would have been frustrated if I had. Sophie once accused me: "You can't love anybody, you're just looking for experience." I could have answered her that abstention from love *is* experience, possibly even more profound than love because there's nothing to fall away from, there is no fear. But this is the mantra of the non-achiever—to make a conquest out of a flaw, a moral stance from an accident or inaction. Maybe the constant quest was better.

Maybe what men really need is merely a story to be in, and if we are obedient to that story, how it turns out is not our responsibility, we become part of a great narrative machine, emblematic and passive. As Chang Tzu said, the world is alright as it is. We serve the future, we serve the species, we serve the physics. But we must *play* our role to do so. Passivity *is* action. But then that didn't make sense either. And the more I drank the more confusing it got. Indeed, I could hear her voice: "You're just using the world like a library, constructing some dramatic myth of yourself, complete with choruses, arias and grand set pieces. But you're no magnet of grandeur. You're small."

That was cruel. And I *was* in a grand set, I thought, but that's easy enough to buy your way into, especially when there's no heroism to factor in. There *was* an endless Bollywood soundtrack, the Qawwali prayer chants, the cries of various vendors, the numerous barking dogs and rumbling wagons, the jackals of the urban forest, and the grunts and squeals of all the other working, rutting and scavenging beasts. I made a note of my surroundings as I stared out the window of the Rava because it would be the last time I would see such surroundings.

As dusk came to Falkland Road, I could tell that people were coming by the bar just to look at me, like a zoo animal, encaged in a failed Orientalist fantasy. I finished my beer and split. I was in a state of minor genital pain by then and that made walking awkward. I didn't know if the people on the street sympathized with my condition or thought I was a fool. The red and yellow powders were still on my face—I was a marked man, a painted bird. Amongst the jeers and street noise, though, I thought I heard someone call my name in a voice I seemed to recognize from a thousand years in the past. But I paid no attention. I knew there was no reality left to me other than my own obsessions, and so I turned my head briefly toward some abstract camera for a final pose. Flash. Captured. Lost.

(thirteen)

Time is plastic and relative both to the situation and the perceiver. What seems like hours to one person goes by as minutes to another. If you're late for work or a date, the second hand fairly races, highlighting your incompetence. If you're hoping the boring social obligation will end soon, the second hand crawls; you can count to ten for every second that passes. Some people live through several major life events in the time it takes others to make a sandwich or buy the ticket.

It was quite some time before I got back to Chicago, stuck as I was in a kind of spiritual gravity hole of self-doubt, depression and overstimulation. I can't say specifically what I did or where I went. I had no ties, no pets, no apartment. I was free to murder the hours and days as they passed. I was in no hurry to get back, and I didn't know what I would say to people when I did. But that day did come. I arrived at the Chicago Greyhound station. I rented a room that was definitely not a hotel room, which must have signaled some kind of commitment. Eventually, I got around to calling Berny. She was a little pissed.

"Jerk," she said.

"Sorry, I did call though." It was true, I had called her a couple of times, but the conversations were short.

As it turned out, Berny had moved into one of my old residences, cattycorner to the St. Boniface graveyard. She could meditate on the gravestones out her window. It made her life intense, she said, because without death there was no pleasure or morality. Infinite time means only infinite procrastination, therefore death was behind everything that was active and good, and Berny liked the constant reminder. It was a real estate *momento mori*, she said, a rentable version of wearing a skull tied to your waist. I went along with it; then we went out to dinner—a Thai joint, not fancy but beyond my current means. "Don't worry she said, I've been working pretty regular."

"Yeah? Doing what?"

"Well, there's only two ways of making a living these days, marketing and humiliation. You should know that," she said, lifting a forkful of squid to her purpled lips. I watched the shriveled tentacles disappear behind her white teeth. Then I watched a guy a few tables away pushing his fork against his palm with unnecessary force. My mind drifted to an old chipped straight razor I had at home. Then Berny asked me what I was thinking. I said "nothing," which was a lie, cause I was thinking of that razor's potential to inflict pain.

Berny said she was copyediting for an S&M magazine, or maybe it was an automobile trade publication. I can't remember, besides there isn't much difference, one was just more obvious. "Anyway, I quit a month or so ago. But it was good money for awhile."

"If it was good money why did you quit?"

"I started to feel sorry for them, I mean the other porn workers, and then I felt sorry for the porn readers, and then I felt sorry for the world at large. Then I started to feel sorry for myself by extension. It just went on and on; I became a great rolling empathy machine. Then I got angry at myself for living in such a sorry-ass world. Then I was disappointed in myself for being angry and then I was sorry for being disappointed. My boyfriend got tired of this circle of pity—it was taking up too much of his mental energy. Figures, right?"

"You didn't tell me you had a boyfriend." She saw my surprise but let it go. In all the time I had known Berny I never knew her to actually be involved with anyone. Romance was always in the past—a story from long ago, something she rarely spoke of.

"You didn't ask," she said. "It's been, what, almost a year? More than that, probably."

"Really? Doesn't seem that long to me."

"Anyway, that was Andreas. You don't know him. He put up with me as long as I was buying food. But his taste changed when the checks stopped coming. Suddenly I wasn't so unique. Neither of us really gave a damn."

"And then?"

"Then what? As someone who forthrightly hates humanity, what could I do, I went back to the Humane Society." She laughed a little.

"Ha ha. I get it."

"Sounds funny, right? I asked for my old job back." She laughed a little more. "But what's really funny is that they gave it to me." She paused as if deciding whether to go on with the story—apparently the answer was no. "Christ, it's like the nineties already. I thought the eighties would last forever. How was New York, anyway?"

That's right. On my way back from India, I had stopped in New York to visit old friends, part of the spiritual drift thing. I had called her from there, so she knew.

"The food is bland, and the women are only interested in your back."

"Ouch. Do I detect a note of bitterness?"

"Detect what you want. A lot of people like the hype. Not me."

"Guess not, huh?" she said, looking rather doubtful. She was sweating now, and took a drink of water.

"This collective need for punishment is getting out of hand," I said. "It's as if the whole culture were feeling guilty for letting itself down." I was picking at some shredded fried pork with chili peppers, knowing I was courting pain—buying into the attitude I had just condemned.

Berny changed the subject as if to avoid agreeing with me: "Yeah. Hey, Kathe had her baby, you know. It's a boy. She named it Ogden." She saw my question coming. "No, not Nash, Utah—Odgen, Utah, where the conception took place."

"Never mind, I'm not going to ask. You and her are still friends?"

"Oh sure. You'll see her tomorrow, probably." She looked away for a few seconds—toward some sound in another part of the room, another reality.

"So whatever happened to Arnaud and that whole drama?"

"Only bad news."

"What bad news?"

"Suicide. That's bad, right?"

I hadn't thought much about Arnaud in the last year or so, maybe on purpose, but I put up a show of interest. After all—I had just asked after him. "How?"

"Apparently he was getting transferred, and some dumbass guard, well, anyway he got himself in front of a bathroom mirror without cuffs on and he broke the glass, and, well you can guess."

"Oh god."

"I think he'd been suicidal all along, but you know in prison they won't let you die, that's the punishment. They make you remain in the world and suffer."

"That *is* the point, I suppose—suffering as punishment."

"I'm not for the death penalty mind you, but if people want to exit, they should let them." She waited for some reaction from me, but I didn't give her one. "You know it's funny," she continued, "after all this time, the thing I remember about Arnaud was that he had this, something like an oral fixation, and was always chewing on something, his glasses, pens, pencils. Remember? Especially the frames of his glasses were always covered with tooth marks like diseased wood or something, mounted on that scruffy face of his."

"I barely remember, but now that you mention it..."

"But then what does it say about me—that this is the thing I remember most about him. Sometimes the only thing we remember about people are such small details. They become the repository of the person's whole personality."

This would have been a good time to bring up the serpent tattoos, and the imaginary plot I had formulated, but I didn't see how it really affected anything anymore. Arnaud had once been a Promethean figure, Satanic even, like a Balzac statue in our minds. We had debated ideas of murder, transcendence, crime, transgression and monstrous acts of will, using him as a catalyst. Now, acts of will seemed less an issue; life was really just a series of mistakes—someone screws up, then redefines their fallen state as exactly what they wanted in the first place. It's all fall, that's all it is. But I didn't say any of this, I just sort of stared off into space for a minute or two.

"Ever hear from Sophie?" Berny asked. "She never showed up around here. There was a rumor she was in L.A., but I was out there a few months ago and I didn't run into anybody that knew her. That's just to be expected, I guess but..."

"Nah, I don't see her in California," I said, "She's not cut out for the automobile lifestyle."

"Yeah, and I called her parents once or twice too. Her sister tells me that, 'Oh she's fine and she is living in London,' or something. At least that's what she thought. But I was sure I heard someone in the background, some guy trying to get her off the phone. It was weird. Then, the second or third time I called, her mother came on, and she seemed pretty upset or pissed off, like why did I keep calling her, you know. They actually told me not to call again, like I was some kind of bad influence in her life or something." Berny paused. "Anyway, this was all a while ago now."

"You're not alone there, I don't think they like me much either." I paused. "I don't understand how she could just disappear like that."

"We don't know that she did disappear. She's probably living next door, or five blocks over."

"Yeah, right."

"But a lot of things *are* disappearing," Berny said, "they have to. Anyway, I was just wondering," she looked closely at me for a second, squinting her eyes theatrically in a way that Sophie often did, then backed off. "Relax. I won't ask." She paused again, then asked, "Anyone else?"

I laughed. "Somehow life's just not living up to the rock & roll soundtrack."

"I feel exactly the same. In fact, I always said the great problem in the world today is the lack of a proper soundtrack. No, I take that back. Actually, I think there are too many soundtracks. Why do we need a soundtrack anyway? First, it's confusing, then, it's dictatorial. No one can get together on it."

"Maybe, but I'd be glad to have a soundtrack at this point, just for the relief, if not for the instruction."

*

It had been awhile since we had seen each other and neither of us showed our true years. Berny was only slightly heavier in the face and thighs. I must have seemed different too, but I didn't know how. We both believed we would evolve into stereotypes *by choice*. I wanted to be The Eccentric Urban Dandy. I'd wear a checkered sport coat and a stingy-brim, pick a street in some city, proclaim myself mayor, run a newsstand, let the kids think I was a freak, pontificate on this and that, tape poetry to lamp posts. Bernadette could go one of two directions: some version of the standard Pigeon-Feeding-Shopping-Bag-Cat-Lady living in a single room, or The Old Broad, a painted has-been with an eternal cigarette and a rocks-glass in her hand—the one who used to be an actor, a dancer, a singer, an artist even, but now she runs a bordello or a bar or just a costume shop. She would be the one that the cops call on when they need a clue about the ways ambition and lust use people.

It seemed ironic or sad because here we were creating idealized images of failure to replace our real ones. Berny and Sophie had fallen out over such matters of personal presentation and so they saw each other as phonies at the same time. And then each began to feel that her special phony image was being used by the other. It was like an emotional property rights dispute. Bernadette claimed to have no understanding of people whose ethics were based on the construction of an image, which she undoubtedly felt was true of Sophie, who, Berny claimed, was truly seduced by her own tragic delusions of grandeur.

"But, she was *your* friend," I protested in reaction

to the unstated conversation. "Or was it really just the entertainment value?"

"They're the same thing aren't they?"

"That's cynical," I said, lighting a smoke with a cynical affectation.

"Yeah maybe, but ain't it like that with all our so-called 'friends'. They engage us because they entertain us, either through flattery or discovery. It's not a negative judgment. Sophie had something we don't have. And we were happy to bear witness. In the end, it's just one more thing to make you sad."

"True enough." I said. Still, I got the feeling that Bernadette was glad Sophie wasn't around anymore, partly because she projected more into her than she was willing to admit. She saw Sophie as some kind of unchanging spirit-of-change, a hyper-tuned receiver of energies that she herself was not privy to, or at least was too preoccupied to acknowledge. More important, Sophie was adaptable for that very reason, and Berny wasn't. I wasn't either. According to Berny, we were crystallizing, me and her, like dinosaurs, into some inescapable version of ourselves and that's why we needed an alternative goal to alleviate our sadness.

"Wait, who said *I was* sad?" I feigned indignity.

"C'mon Frank. You're miserable and you know it. I can hear the fucking misery cogs grinding away in your brain. It's as loud as the el train going around a corner. That's why you don't have any friends. The noise scares them off."

"Thanks." She was joking, I knew, but it was true,

I didn't have any friends. Sophie had been my friend. In fact, I actually missed the arguing, "Who will I fight with?"

"Argue with me. You know you can," she said. "But maybe you don't want to. But seriously, I got nothing else to do. I'll be your Sophie." She shrugged at the submissive status this might suggest.

"It wouldn't be the same," I said.

I realized then that Sophie was the only person against whom I could fashion myself in contrast. Which could mean that I secretly really wanted to oppose her, which might also mean that I didn't really love her. But I didn't want to go there—it would ruin my narrative.

Then I noticed a black spot in Berny's eye, something like a bullet seen from a great distance. At first I thought that bullet might be an accusation, but then I realized it was more; it was something like the whole condensed code of the role Berny had formed for me to play, but it was shaped like a bullet. It would be painful to play that role, too, because I knew I was something completely different to Bernadette than I was to myself.

It was equally true that Sophie, as we referred to her, was also the product of our projections. And so, as we remembered her, we changed her to fit what *we were now*, not what we were when we knew her. We also knew that if Sophie ever did make it back to Chicago, she would simply be somebody else—broken, triumphant, self-righteous, self-deluded, maybe even introverted—a whole new woman in a whole new world. There was no sense thinking we would, or ever could, know her again. She might not even know herself. She might have become the kind of person she hated. A lot of people did. I also think that what people hate or find fault with in others is what they most fear in themselves—that looming inevitability. And then, there's the pressure to avoid it. And that attempt to avoid the fate is what actually forces the fate to manifest itself in the end. Fearing *it* makes *it* true.

"Look, I was wondering, Frank, I know for a fact you weren't over in India all that long. I mean, did you even look for her?" I was about ready to admit that I had not looked for her, but Berny answered for me. "No. You didn't look and I know why—because it was all really about you, not her; you used the story as a crisis scenario around which you built some little drama of redemption, some way to excuse yourself.

"But I did think of her. And I did go there. That's something."

"Not really. It's not that much. You did it for yourself."

"It was enough for me, and maybe for her, too. If she wanted to be found there would be a way."

"Possibly. Look, everything is not just possible, everything is actual; it is all actually happening all the time. Scientists are proving this is true—it's the 'multiple universes' theory of space/time. In order to observe something, like your own life, let's say, you have to impose a set, or framework of rules, and it's that framework that creates the world you see. That's why religious people have visions. They see God everywhere.

Atheists don't see God at all."

I said, "You're wrong. I'm an atheist and I have visions."

"No you don't, you have imagination," she said. "It's different."

There was a long pause. "Funny how the plot just sort of fizzles out," she said, pouring a little beer on the table-top and watching the foam. "It sort of disappears when you try to chase it down, doesn't it?"

"That's not true," I said, "It gets more complicated the more you look into it. That fizzling out is really the resolution of the one grand plot into thousands of subplots, new plots, newer littler stories about less important things—more complicated but less grand."

"Well, that's true too."

*

We were on our second iced coffee and wired. The waiter wanted us to leave. The kitchen staff was cleaning noisily. We ignored them. "So, ah, any 'projects' these days?" I asked, trying not to sound too cynical.

She smiled, "Since you ask."

She then launched into a stream of thought I had difficulty following. One of Berny's favorite topics had always been mass media as collective unconscious and the way individuals learned to imitate it and the consequences of the feedback loop it created. It followed that the role of theater was not only a formula by which to act, but also a kind of emotional voyeurism, the idea being to "feel" emotions without having any responsibility for them. Then she jumped to S&M, which was too Catholic, and besides physical pain was a cheap way out. Then she jumped again to the idea that because Christian women believe they are "condemned" to pain, they pass that burden to their children, whose pain becomes the mother's relief, which in turn creates her guilt. Why, she asked, do you think the newborn cries? It just goes on and on, with the death agony and the wail of the mourners as the last link in this circle of screams.

"This is getting depressing," I said.

"Well, you see," she said, "you make it work for you."

"And I suppose you are?"

"That's what I'm getting at, the new 'project,' as you so generously put it. Here it was: she had recorded Kathe's birth cries, and made a tape that matched the score of Tristan & Isolde. You could do that now with computers, and they had a friend in a studio who had some access. Berny had edited the tape so that at certain points it exactly re-created the *leibestod* and at others it was broken up into a kind of scat singing, a modern *bel canto*, as she called it. After all, what better soundtrack for these times than some overwrought, urgent dithering. You could do other things too: if you sped up the tape, it could sound like gunfire, or swarming bees, or you could slow it down to sound like the sea. Our reality was exactly relative to speed.

An image of Berny as a mad woman in a rocking

chair came into my head.

It was a little like appreciating abstract art, she went on, you had to have this framing device in your head, a predisposition or prejudice. You just matched it up: an argument, an accident, a crime, a couple of queens singing show tunes, a midget doing handstands. She would hang out on Wilson and Broadway armed with a video camera and a boombox, playing this tape, scripting the scene in her head. She could be as elaborate and wacked out as she wanted to be, because it was all her and no one else could see it; they could only suspect it. That's what made everybody schizophrenic, you see, because nobody knew who they really were, because who they were was a character in someone else's play, in this case, *her* play, and she could change their role at will.

"I do it for the feeling of control," she said. "Of course, I'm in their play too, even if they don't think of it that way. But I do, and that makes me schizophrenic to the nth."

I was just staring at her now, and she felt defensive. "Hey! I may be schizo, but at least I'm solvent," she said, motioning for the check. "Besides, all anybody really wants to do is eat and have sex. And you can't have sex anymore without dying maybe."

"Didn't Philip Marlowe say that?" I asked.

"Yeah . . . but I think it was for different reasons."

(fourteen)

It was the 17th of September, one day after the "death-day" of Maria Callas and there had been some kind of special on TV which Berny had taped. She called me over and Kathe came by too, with liquor and cigarettes and the baby, Ogden. They were going to watch the tape and figure out ways to manipulate it. We all went down to Solomon's store to use his VCR because it was in better shape.

"Yesterday was Sophie's birthday, you know," I said.

"You're right, I forgot. Poor Sophie. Hey, we ought to have a party. The two occasions will cancel each other out."

"Of course."

The program was a compilation of concert footage from the 50s and 60s, mostly Paris, mostly on stage at the Palais Garnier. Though I was surprised by what I saw, I'm not sure why. Maria Callas was simply an image to be used for our pleasure, as any image is used. Of course, some strictly post-modern materialist might say the image of Callas *used us*—to augment itself, to grow stronger and perhaps to conquer. I don't know. I didn't really know much about her. Despite her reputation, she looked sick in the video, as opposed to vicious or arrogant. She looked like an aged butterfly whose voice was a pleading, vaguely metallic, attack on a world that had failed her. The thin neck and sharp strained features, the jaw, nose and over-large eyes, all features of a heavier woman, were exaggerated by the gangly, expensive jewelry hanging from her face and limbs like fruit, drawing our attention, not to her glamour, but to her frailty. Indeed, there was a clownish, bird-like quality to her that led us into a conversation about Freud, physicality and sound.

It started with Kathe saying something about the navel gazing of artists and intellectuals. Berny then launched into what seemed less a defense than a planned speech.

"Freud said there was a place in every dream, a drain where the whole thing fails. That's where the dream communicates with the greater universe. Failure is the key. You can stare at your own naval but you can't stare at the dream naval, just as you can't stare at God's face if you want to remain whole. And you can't stare into the mouth of Maria Callas when she hits her high A or E or whatever. It's too vaginal, and it can, like a birth scream," Berny made some strange hand gesture, "act as the passage between creation and nothingness. Perhaps this accounts for the public fear of divas, as well as the transcendental effects attributed to their hokey performances." She laughed. I tried to laugh along with her. "God is nothing but an acoustic hallucination," she said.

Berny went on, advocating a kind of pan-religious phoneme mysticism that could be found in Kabalistic incantation, for example, or in the sacred Ka Ra Kee Cho syllables of the Hermetic Caduceus, or in the Om Hrim Strim Hum Phat mantra of Tantric Spiritualism and Durga worship, or in the Primal Despairing Moan of Ontological Existentialism. She spoke of the New Guinea Kaluli who thought you could hear the universe weeping in birdsong. She spoke of certain Hindu cults in which Siva's great squeaking three-piece heart supposedly gave forth the fifty tones of consciousness and sorrow from which all symphonies are wrought. She spoke of the primal *Langue de Oiseaux*, sought by certain occultists, a language that had no dictionary or syntax.

I tried to interject here with something about sonic alchemy and transformation but Berny was on a roll and would let no one interrupt her. Yes, she said, it was all birdspeak and heartbreak and even Kali herself could be thought of less as a graveyard prostitute or a perfect wife to ascetics and masochists and more as a decadent vowel that resides in the center of all sonar experience. Could the 300 reputed voices of Maria Callas therefore be compared to an aviary, or the degrading fragments of that primal vowel?

At this point, even though I knew her speechifying was something of a joke, I also thought it might not be good for Berny to be alone for long periods of time. These thoughts however, did not slow her down.

Would it be possible, she continued, to graph certain "holy" notes against their natural or esoteric counterparts—to map Italian *bel canto* onto New Guinea birdsong or a Karnataka mantra onto the howling of the feral Humbolt Park dogs? Berny delivered her questions with a chuckle at the absurdity of it, which I got.

On the other hand, I was a little surprised that such absurdity was laced with what seemed to be a Sonny Valentine-style occultism. But then it's all just a circle of repeating ideas that no one ever really gets, because if you really *get it*, then it isn't really there anymore, or rather, it may be there but it becomes useless—the aggression of your understanding degrades it. Still, as atheists, all we had was the physical world and we had to make something out of it.

So Berny rewound the tape and played it back pausing and rewinding again at specific scenes. Like a sinister Professor Moreau, using a snapped-off automobile antenna for a pointer, she commented on the singer's repertoire of mannerisms, which she claimed spanned the animal gamut from reptile to child, from Mediterranean Audrey Hepburn to Good Friday Jackie O. It wasn't really acting she did, though, it was channeling—the theatrical pretension of the eyes, the backwards look over the shoulder, the feigned innocence, the coyness, the fake surprise, all while periodically hugging herself, as if always cold, like an orphan on a train. It was a catalogue of gestures passed down through the ages that could be traced back in time to a single primitive moment of presentation when the birth of theater and self-consciousness were the same.

It dawned on me that this was all a kind of rehearsal for a performance piece that Berny had in mind, which like most of her performance pieces, she would never actually perform, except for us. But she was doing a good job of mocking professorial pretension with snake oil, and we said so.

Stagecraft was something women learn to do early, she said, they figure out the lighting and angles and how to work them. Ultimately, there are some things they can't control—myth always bleeds through, or at least it appropriates the disinterested subject matter for its own use. During a particular Rossini scene, Berny exclaimed "Note, how the shallow focus of the camera made the chorus behind the diva seem like a James Ensor-like tableau of carnival masks at a public shaming, desperate for something to pronounce upon.

"Note, as well, the curious separation," Berny proclaimed while pointing to the TV screen with her antenna, "the way the voice separates out above the audience, while the singer is left abandoned on stage." This disembodied effect was, of course, heightened not only by the poor tape quality but also by the fact the film was old to begin with. The sound seemed to have separated slightly from the visual, giving it a decayed or dubbed quality.

Of course, once the effect had been pointed out, it could be noticed even in our close quarters. Berny and the others separated from their voices, then faded into the background while my own thoughts and observations came into deeper relief. I started to think about how all the people in these operas were actually dead and that the image I was seeing was nothing but a trace, a scratch on the surface of a material reality, a residue of silver powders or magnetized iron dust. But what's more important is, realizing that Callas died back in

1977, I somehow remembered knowing about it, even being present for the news, which surprised me. Indeed, I *was* in Paris in '77. Yes, I was sure of it. I remembered the event because I was sleeping in a park. I forget which one, Parc Monceau, maybe. And the news of her death was the headline of the paper I was using for a pillow—Figaro, or Le Monde or Le Parisian. *"Maria Anna Sophie Cecilia Kalogeropoulos, dite la Callas, a toujours suscité les passions.* I could not read the paper and I did not know who she was at the time, I only knew the name, the image.

Another thing that struck me was a scene from Tosca: everything around the diva was black—the darkness of the background against which she moved was a fluid darkness massing its inky bulk into clouds of varying density. This darkness was not exactly the cremation ground of Kali's erotic dance as I had pictured it, but a kind of black consuming fire just the same. It swirled around the singer, as if attracted by her fragility. Maybe it was precisely the pressure of this darkness that pressed out the arias and the farcical physical expressions that everyone loved.

Then another thing happened. Maybe it was just a bad taping, or an effect of the VCR not working properly, but the screen was taken over for a few seconds by a whitish static from which the image of the woman in the white gown, dancing erratically, seemed to struggle to relieve itself, and I realized that this was an image I'd seen before. It was as if the icon was playing behind the surfaces, waiting for opportunities to manifest herself in my unimportant life. Indeed, at least at this moment, the diva had become an aural and visual attractor for all the random images and signs I might assemble into this fiction called my little life. And, oddly, I also thought that possibly Sophie was related to this struggle between assembly and decay, especially if you could say each woman was destroyed or devoured by what they thought was their heart's desire.

Berny always said divinity corrupts and that it was divinity that destroyed most people, because when you call upon the spirit of an icon to bolster your own mediocre presence in this world—be it goddess, movie star, or whoever—you are trading on a commodity that begins to lose value the minute it is acquired. And furthermore, those academic populists who attempt to justify celebrity worship by relating it to ancient mythical figures are merely rationalizing what Berny called spiritual laziness. *That*, she could forgive, but not irresponsible attributions of divinity. In her opinion, the bogus cult of the goddess did nothing but render women inert, forcing them into a negative double bind. What happens, for instance, when the "chosen one" is forced to ask herself, "Who am I to deprive these starving masses of what they need?" No one inquires after the loneliness of that decision, or the inner conflict caused by arrogance and simultaneous submission. This all goes to explain why, Berny said, when they tried to throw Maria's ashes in the sea, they blew back in everyone's face—such is the judgment of the dead. But such also is our complicity in the flaws of others.

"What do you mean by that?" Kathe asked, doubting Berny's progressive direction.

"I mean these people don't exist without us. We are complicit in the ego of someone like Callas, just as we are complicit in the violence of Kali or the virginity of Mary, or the tragedy of Janis and Jimi. We are also complicit in the so-called mystery of Sophie. No one is what they are without their place in the stories of their friends and their enemies. In fact, you don't even know who you are really, outside of your own limited perceptions."

*

I felt drained and dumb. So I went back to my room and took my regular sedative. I fell asleep and had myself a dream: I was a boy in a cabin that seemed to be adrift in a howling storm. Outside were vast plains, distant mountains and a full moon—it was classic spaghetti-gothic with an appropriately disturbing soundtrack—the howling of a pack of Sergio Leone dogs as they galloped across the landscape, chasing shadows. I went to the window to watch the dogs, and was suddenly aware that someone was speaking. The woman speaking was beside and slightly behind me, with her lips close to my ear, but I could not see her, though I did see a vague white reflection in the glass. This reflection seemed to form hesitantly, then dissolve, then reform, and then dissolve again. I had the feeling she had always been there, but I also knew if I turned around she would disappear. "When you hear the howling of the dogs in the countryside," she said, "don't hide under your covers. It is merely an insatiable thirst that drives them." Then the viewpoint changed and I was no longer in the floating room; I was on the street looking up at my own window where a woman, standing beside a boy, was drawing the blind aside as she stared off into the distance. This time she looked a lot like Sophie, and I could hear her, and it was Sophie's voice and she was holding a book and reciting to me, "I too feel this yearning," she said. "And I cannot satisfy the hunger. They tell me I am the daughter of a man and a woman. This astounds me," she said, "I thought I was more."

In an early tale of Kali, from the Jaiminiya Brahmana, the goddess goes by the name Long-Tongue. One day she is confronted by the hero Sumitra who would seduce her for her soma. She intimidates him with a thousand hungry vaginas, and the only way he could conquer her was by filling each one. So Indra granted handsome Sumitra one thousand penises in exactly the right locations. He then returned to the forest and had intercourse with the horrid demon, and in this manner Long-Tongue was immobilized, pinned down to the world in a thousand places. The story ends with this epithet: "To keep the pressed drink at its best and most intoxicating, my friends, pierce away the long-tongued dog."

EPILOGUE

I read somewhere that the human heart can be thought of as an organ of passage, the path to a no-man's land of astonishment and submission, or isolation and freedom. Our choice is either to balance on this threshold in absolute stillness and beatitude, or to fall away in any direction. But that fall is always into speed, into time. The Kali Yuga is said to be a subtle thing—it is not simply an era, but a quality of time, and, of course, of the heart. Wherever the heart is impure, *that* is the Kali Yuga. It can be right down the street. It can be in your mind.

I often try to avoid revelations when they threaten my emotional balance. Like most men, I simply do what I have to do: I go to the bathroom, I wash the dishes, I putter about my room rearranging magazines and pens. I avoid looking out the window at the bridges and the stars. I know they are out there but I am uncomfortable with the idea of using them as vehicles of transformation. I don't trust myself; I don't trust where I might end up. My heart is not ready, nor is it large. But the world trickles in through tiny fissures anyway.

I could never stop replaying the memory of certain events, as if they composed a toy city in my mind, a little sinister landscape, and in the little sinister streets of a city in that landscape live all my little personal characters, like wind-up dolls ready to be activated, ready to go through their given roles of blame and rejection. It was an appropriately small theater invented by me for my own redemption, but all it really did was torture me like a calliope that wouldn't stop.

*

Of course, I did (and still do) claim to have some kind of tape machine in my head, and with said machine, I could walk down Falkland Road again and again, repeating at my pleasure, that scene of so many months previous. The characters would basically be the same, but sometimes they would change. People from whole other time periods and stories would make guest appearances: abandoned women, bad father figures of the road, hostile friends. There were celebrities, too, and game show hosts from "You Bet Your Life." Bhairavi was there, and her doorway in the dream world had acquired a neon sign proclaiming, "Multiple Personalities Our Specialty." It was true too, especially of her. Sometimes she was a clever man offering purple anti-depressants or glassine envelopes full of white powder. Sometimes she was a gruff bartender stealing away the spring of my life. Sometimes her face was composed of cut-up maps of old roads like wires, all humming out there with bad ideas.

I could walk those roads all the way back to that hotel room in Benares, where Sophie's sickness was so acute. She was thinner then. She had become, in fact, a strip of white paper with penciled-on eyes and some wavy lines indicating limbs. But suffering should pull people together. And I swear I was only applying her standards that night in August when I became patronizing. "That's not love," she said, "that's guilt." There was no way to answer that. We were always talking past each other, towards some other goal. Answers were useless and questions had motives.

Helplessness is often said to make a claim on love; people have used it against each other for years. Sophie had accused me of finding her weakness attractive. Did I? Did I love her more because she was ill, or because she suffered? Did I love her because she was divided against herself? Was she really two uncomfortable people, instead of one? Was her suffering something I projected into her? Perhaps she felt that she would have to suffer in order to have credibility with me. But that idea made me feel guilty, and to this day I believe she was wrong about it. But then again, it's hard to argue my side.

It's funny how, looking back, sometimes, I can't quite picture Sophie in my mind. Other times I think I could easily conjure any number of ideal images of her. One especially remains: a ghostly white figure walking ahead of me on a dark Victorian street. We were in London and the tube had closed. Our friend, Emma Bovary (a stage name), had done a stand-up routine in some bar in Islington that night and she'd given Sophie this white dress to wear as a prop in the performance. Afterwards, we were tired and Sophie decided just to wear it home. I was walking slightly ahead when she accused me of treating her like a Chinese wife. Then I did what I often did—I slowed down until *she* was ahead of *me*. We didn't speak for a minute or two. Then she turned and looked back over her shoulder and gestured with her left arm: "C'mon, catch up."

*

Back in Chicago, the morning after the Berny's Kallas video party, I woke up facing the back of a couch. I felt like a virtual protagonist in that old computer game called "Deja Vue." The agent in the game wakes up in a room; he doesn't know where or who he is and the object of the game is to figure that out. I knew only slightly more than the guy in the game, because at least I knew it *was* a game. I knew I had friends. Things happened in my friends' lives and I was supposedly a part of that. There was Bernadette, Arnaud, Stacey, Boggs, Kathe, and Sophie, each of whom seemed to be following their own divergent scripts.

Arnaud couldn't tell the difference between a metaphor and a spiritual command and he stepped over the line. It's only amazing that it didn't happen earlier. You can get rid of the sign but the signified hangs around; the problem is—you have no way of knowing which is which. The old cliché goes that intercourse puts a man on equal terms with his mother, and violence puts him on a footing with his father. Arnaud had accomplished one, then he wanted the other. Boggs, I suppose, simply went mad. The responsibility for his actions drove him to a state of overwhelming passivity. He moved to Mopetown, a neighborhood no one could find on a map. Emily Dickinson became his role model. Kathe moved in with her girlfriend Edna Millay, a performance artist. Together they would raise the child Ogden as a renaissance man.

And where did Sophie go? Was she an emptiness or a plenitude? Was I falling away from her or chasing her? Would it matter if I knew? Maybe, as she had often said, I took her away from the better life she would have led as a famous person in a bigger, more exciting world. Fair enough. But to say so denied her own will in the situation. And whether she was now a prostitute in some subcontinental brothel, or a swing shift worker in a Southside steel plant, or living large in London, it was, in most respects, a moot point. Time moves forward, the path bifurcates, the doors close as we go, and one wrong-headed belief is about as good as the next. The whole of culture, the entire way of the world, is an accumulation of accidents, fire and collision. We pretend to love the heroes who break through this cage of microcosmic fate, but they are few, and, they are usually made, not products of their own will.

*

Meanwhile here I was—facing another threshold of decision. What to do? Bernadette had said that there should be one thing in your life that you want desperately but force yourself to do without—and with that great renunciation all things become possible. I said that I would renounce women and that I would approach sex as a purely mental phenomenon from then on. That way I could experience all the pain and none of the pleasure. Berny said, renounce sex, okay, but not women. Ritual, she said, ritual is the key.

She herself had taken up the baking of bread, an idea she got from a PBS documentary about life in some French monastery. She claimed it was a highly sexualized endeavor for this reason: the monks put their suppressed libido into the bread (and the brandy). The Virgin Mary was their ideal mate. They enjoyed her in all her sensuous innocence, as it was embodied symbolically in the powdered dough they kneaded. The body of the divine mother was thus transfigured as the most basic form of nourishment. By eating the bread they actively consummated with the Virgin.

Berny and I, however, had no virgins to make. While the bread baked, we sipped single-malt Scotch, made by monk-like Highlanders who never left their peat-bog distilleries except to sing their songs out on the moaning moors.

Bernadette had it all worked out, and if it wasn't all that spiritual, at least it was a distraction, especially from the worldly aspects of her work at the Humane Society, which involved caring for and occasionally killing those sick and forsaken creatures unfit for urban life. In the process she had created what amounted to a little Medical Oddity Museum of the Misbegotten. She had a two-headed kitten in a bottle, a six-legged dog, and something with a wide forehead and three eyes. She said evolution was all accident and that we were headed, every one of us, for eventual corporal dysfunction.

They did a lot of abortions at the Society, usually the result of late spaying. One day Berny gave me a present—a bottle of German Sheppard embryos floating around a plastic Sears Tower. She had put a hand-drawn label on it: A Rain of Plague. If you shook the bottle, the little embryos swirled around like snow. Puppy embryos from heaven, symbols of cuteness and purity, floating down around the Sears Tower, symbol of human hubris—that's how she described it. It's funny, she said, because dogs and early humans evolved together as homeless wanderers.

I didn't know how it was funny, but as I shook the bottle and watched the embryo-snow, I noticed that Berny had some Maria Callas record playing on the stereo. It had probably been playing the entire time but I was only, at that moment, aware of it. "*Cielo! dove son io? Che veggio! ah! per pieta, non mi svegliate voi,*" and this was followed by a chorus of whispery howls, and I could not tell if they were dogs or opera singers. I did not know where in the world we were, but I felt we must be sleep-walking through our lives.

I looked at Bernadette and she looked back. Something washed over us both like a solution in a dark-room fixing pan, trying to freeze us in time. It was an invitation that we had to reject. But in doing so, I exposed myself ever so briefly to what must have been the great wheel of being—a fire-eyed, eight-spoked spider wheel rolling around and around inside a larger twelve-spoked wheel, itself rolling inside the ten directions of an indifferent sky that never ages. There is no time or location. It does not depart and it does not arrive. And I could never describe why or where such an image came from, nor the vague elation I felt upon receiving it. I didn't know what to say then and I still don't. Frank Payne never seems to know what to say. And yet he talks to himself all the time.

By the way, I think I still have that homemade embryo snow globe. Well, I don't actually *have* it with me. It's in a box in someone's attic—someone who no longer talks to me, probably.

Carl Watson is a poet, fiction writer, playwright and critic. He grew up in Northwest Indiana and has since lived in Portland Oregon, New Orleans, Chicago, New York and Paris. He has traveled extensively in India and other parts east of the Atlantic. He currently splits his time between NYC and an old barn in the Catskill Mountains. Watson has written cultural criticism and reviews for various journals including The Village Voice, NY Press, Downtown, Tribes, and The Williamsburg Observer. He is the author of several books of fiction, including *Bricolage ex Machina* (Lost Modern Press), *Beneath the Empire of the Birds* (Apathy Press), *The Hotel of Irrevocable Acts* (Autonomedia), and *Backwards the Drowned Go Dreaming*, a novel published by Sensitive Skin Books. He has also published several collections of poetry, including *Anarcadium Pan* (Erie Street Press), *Living for the Ecstasy Sect, Confessions of an Aspirin Eater, The Green Man* (Apathy). His latest collection, *Astral Botanica*, is published by Fly by Night Press, the imprint of A Gathering of the Tribes. He has been published in various journals including Sensitive Skin, The Brooklyn Rail, Evergreen Review, Degraphe, Liberation and others.

The novel *Hotel des acts irrevocables* (Gallimard) and the short story collections *Sous l'empire des oiseaux, la vie psychosomatique, and Hank Stone et le coeur de craie* (vagabonde) have been published in France. Vagabonde press will publish the novel *Backwards the Drowned Go Dreaming* in 2016.

Watson received the Kathy Acker Award for Fiction in 2012.

Watson wrote his Ph.D. dissertation on the autobiography of the outsider artist, Henry Darger. He continues to work with Darger's manuscripts while publishing articles about his work. He teaches literature in the CUNY system, most recently at Baruch College.

ROOTS & BRANCHES SERIES TITLES ARE MADE POSSIBLE
IN PART THROUGH THE GENEROUS CONTRIBUTIONS OF

Thaddeus Rutkowski
Lynzee
Lori J. Anderson-Moseman
Richard Martin
Lee Slonimsky
Elayna Browne
Kenneth B. Nemcosky
Barbara Henning
Katy Masuga
James A. Reiss
Elizabeth J. Coleman
K Feather Hastings
Susan Lewis
Michael Boughn
Karen Gunderson
William Luvaas
Stephen Sartarelli
Maximilian W. Valerio
Andrea Scrima
Lewis Warsh
Vitaly Chernetsky
Kathy Conde
j/j hastain
Andrew K Peterson
Marc Estrin
Gloria Frym
Marc Vincenz
Michael Forstrom